Mistletoe With a Pink Bow

A Witch's Cove Mystery
Book 8

Vella Day

Mistletoe With a Pink Bow
Copyright © 2020 by Vella Day
Print Edition
www.velladay.com
velladayauthor@gmail.com

Cover Art by Jaycee DeLorenzo
Edited by Rebecca Cartee and Carol Adcock-Bezzo

Published in the United States of America

Print book ISBN: 978-1-951430-24-5

ALL RIGHTS RESERVED. No part of this book may be used or reproduced in any manner whatsoever without written permission of the author except in the case of brief questions embodied in critical articles or reviews.

This is a work of fiction. Names, characters, places, and incidents either are the product of the author's imagination or are used fictitiously, and any resemblance to actual persons living or dead, business establishments, events or locales, is entirely coincidental.

A witchy time travel tale that could only happen to me—and on Christmas Eve no less.

Hi, I'm Glinda Goodall. I know I'm a witch, but I never expected to have my powers turn against me and send me and Jaxson back fifty years to a snowy winter wonderland. Who knew the seventies were so archaic? No computers, no cell phones, and TVs with small screens that weighed as much as a battleship. Okay, gas might have been $.36 a gallon, but that seemed to have been the only plus.

Experiencing what it was like way back then was fun for about one day, but wouldn't you know it, a guest is murdered in the old Victorian B&B where we are staying. Surprise! Adding insult to injury, the only way we can return to sunny Witch's Cove in the 21st century is to solve this murder case—or so says some psychic.

I'll be honest, at first it kind of sounded fun, until I wondered how could we do that with no modern conveniences and no gossip queens? Even worse, there was no email.

Please send all suggestions my way, though I have no idea if they will ever reach me. Oh, yeah. I'll be the girl in the bell bottom jeans that aren't even pink. Such indignities.

Chapter One

"WHAT DO YOU think?" I held up a sprig of mistletoe tied together with a pink bow.

My cousin Rihanna laughed. "Where do you plan to put that?"

I shouldn't be surprised she acted as if mistletoe was some old-fashioned tradition. After all, she was just a teenager. I personally thought it was romantic, yet I was nine years older than she. "In Jaxson's house. We're spending Christmas Eve there."

"Okay, I'll admit that does sound like fun." Thankfully, she seemed sincere.

"And you? Do you and Gavin have plans?"

My cousin and Gavin Sanchez, an intern in his mother's medical examiner practice, had been dating for about three months. Rihanna was eighteen and technically an adult, so I never questioned her about their relationship. She was a very pretty girl who had turned into a self-confident young woman since moving here, and Gavin was bright and focused.

"He's taking me out to dinner to some place in Ocean View. It's supposed to be quite nice." She smiled and then sighed.

I was happy for her. She'd not had the easiest upbringing.

When she moved to Witch's Cove, Florida, from across the state four months ago, she'd been sullen, rebellious, and withdrawn, but I understood why she was unhappy. My aunt had not been a good role model, especially after Rihanna's father disappeared when my cousin was only a year old. He reemerged sixteen years later, and because of Uncle Travis' sudden appearance, Aunt Tricia decided to go into rehab. From what my mother told me, Rihanna's mom would be released in a few weeks.

What my cousin's next step would be, I wasn't sure, but I didn't want her to leave, that was for sure. Between Jaxson and me—and Gavin, of course—I hoped she'd choose to stay, at least until she finished her senior year of high school. If she wanted to make Witch's Cove her permanent home after that, I, for one, would be thrilled.

"That sounds wonderful," I said. "Don't forget we are due at my parents' place tomorrow at noon to open some presents and then have Christmas dinner."

"I'll remember; don't worry."

My mom had invited Gavin and his mother, too, since Elissa's in-laws would be out of town visiting their son in Miami. Naturally, I wanted Jaxson to be with us, but he'd already committed to going back home with his brother, Drake. Because Jaxson's younger brother was the one to visit their parents on a semi-regular basis, Jaxson felt the need to be there at least on Christmas Day. He'd steered clear of his folks for many years due to some bad choices he'd made growing up—and for being falsely imprisoned for a few years.

Iggy, my fifteen-year-old pink iguana familiar crawled out from under the sofa, wearing a green hoodie, one of the early

Christmas presents my Aunt Fern had made for him. Even though we lived in Florida, it could get chilly in December, and the office was rather drafty. Being cold-blooded, Iggy needed to stay warm to survive. I had to admit he looked adorable in his spiffy new outfit.

"Christmas is tomorrow. Did you both buy me some presents?" he asked.

I chuckled. "Did you get us anything?" I totally understood it was a ridiculous comment, but I didn't want him to be any more entitled than he already was.

"Maybe."

From the way he averted his gaze, that was a hard no. Footsteps sounded on the interior staircase from the wine and cheese shop below. That would be Jaxson Harrison, my business partner in our new venture, The Pink Iguana Sleuths. Yes, Iggy's ego soared because of that title.

I smiled, happy every time I saw him. "Hey."

"Ready to grab that bite?" he asked.

"I am." I had already asked Rihanna if she wanted to join us for lunch, but she said she wanted to pick up one more present for Gavin.

Iggy didn't like the cold, so, for once, he was willing to stay back at the office and keep things under control. What he could do if anyone broke in, I didn't know, but he liked being given the responsibility of office protector.

I grabbed my jacket from the back of the sofa and shrugged it on. It might be sixty degrees outside, but for this Florida native girl, that was cold. Please don't judge.

Before I get too far into this narrative, let me introduce myself. I'm Glinda Goodall, a twenty-seven-year-old former math teacher, who decided that I was better suited to being a waitress than dealing with middle schoolers.

After our first town murder happened, however, Jaxson suggested I should open this sleuth agency, mostly because I'm terminally nosy. Naturally, I asked him to join me. I also happen to be a witch, and that particular talent—when my spells actually worked the way they were supposed to—helped solve several crimes. I need to point out that our town is full of psychics, witches, and on occasion, some rogue werewolves. Too often, one needed to fight magic with magic, so to speak.

We were half way to the Tiki Hut Grill when something shiny on the ground caught my attention. Normally, I wasn't the type to pick up a coin, but this particular one was gold-colored, so I bent down and snatched it. Jaxson stopped so we could both look at it. "Have you seen anything like this before?" I flipped it over.

"No. It looks like it came from a game, or else it's some fake doubloon like the ones they toss from balconies or floats during Mardi Gras."

"You're probably right." I was about to drop it when Jaxson grabbed my wrist. "Or it could be a wish coin."

I laughed. "A wish coin? What is that?"

"My grandmother used to say that if you find a coin on the road, pick it up, and make a wish. It just might come true."

"Was grandma big into buying lottery tickets, too?"

He laughed. "Turns out, she was."

I had to assume his grandmother never hit it big. "For grandma, I will give it a try." A gust of wind blew off the Gulf, forcing me to pull my coat tighter. "How about we get to the restaurant first? Besides, I have to think of a wish. I only get one, right?" I wanted to know the Harrison family rules.

He smiled and wrapped a warm and protective arm around my waist. "Yes, you only get one. Come on."

The Tiki Hut, which was owned and run by my Aunt Fern, was surprisingly busy, but we were seated rather quickly. My aunt, who was standing behind the check-out counter, waved. I figured as soon as she finished with the couple who was paying their bill, she'd stop over for a quick chat. We sat down, and I slipped off my jacket.

"What is your wish?" Jaxson asked.

I thought he might have forgotten about it, but he seemed quite serious. I didn't want to pick any subject too deep—like something that involved us—nor did I want to make light of the situation. I wanted to do the coin justice, which meant I wouldn't say I wanted to have someone hand me a million dollars. That wasn't going to happen, wish or no wish.

I looked outside at the rather grayish day to help me decide. Then inspiration struck, and I turned back to Jaxson. "I have it. When I was a little girl, every Christmas Eve I would ask my parents if they could make it snow on Christmas Day. You see, Mom would play all the Christmas classics, especially those by Bing Crosby and Perry Como. Hearing about a white Christmas made both of us rather sentimental, I guess." I placed the coin in my palm and then closed my fist around it. "My wish is to see snow on Christmas."

Jaxson leaned back in his chair. "You do realize that probably won't happen unless we hop in a car and drive north for about fifteen hours."

He was being silly. "I do realize that, but I read it snowed here back in the seventies. It could happen again."

"The forecast for tomorrow calls for temperatures in the seventies."

I shrugged. "A wish is a wish. Don't forget, I am a witch. Maybe it will come true."

Jaxson reached across the table and squeezed my hand. "Dream on, pink lady."

That nickname *pink lady* came about because I only wear pink. Even I didn't know why I did—genetic defect maybe? I shut my eyes and pretended to conjure snow. That was way, way out of my witch abilities, but a girl's gotta try. When a good ten seconds had passed, I opened my eyes. "I realize I've used up the wish on this coin, but if you had one of your own, what would you wish for?"

"Hmm. That is a hard one."

I couldn't believe I was actually holding my breath. Was I hoping he'd say that we could always be together? That was silly, of course. Our relationship had only just begun.

"My wish is that we have a constant stream of clients for our blossoming business."

His choice didn't surprise me. Of the two of us, Jaxson was the practical one. "I hope that comes true as well."

Once we ordered, my aunt came over. "Do you two lovebirds have plans for tonight?"

Lovebirds? I wanted to disappear. Sure, Jaxson and I were a couple, but so far, we'd kept it fairly simple. "We do. I'm envisioning some popcorn, soft music, and a nice warm fire." And some kissing, of course, which was why I planned to take the mistletoe with me. "What are your plans?"

I know my parents had invited her to spend the evening with them, but she also had several of her friends she could be with. Ever since the death of Aunt Fern's last boyfriend, she'd kept to herself. That was a shame, since she used to have an active social life.

"We're having a girls' afternoon over at Miriam's. We'll each bring a gift and have a mini-Christmas party. We have to do it early because Pearl wants to spend some time with her grandson."

"That sounds fun." From the way her eyes were shining, she was quite excited about it. "Who else will be there?"

"The usual crew: Maude, Pearl, Dolly, and myself."

Of course. The five gossip queens. The Pink Iguana Sleuths might not have solved even one case had it not been for their information. It certainly helped that the eldest member, Pearl, was the sheriff's grandmother and worked as his receptionist, despite the fact her hearing was suspect.

Aunt Fern's cell chimed, but being polite, she didn't answer it. "See who it is," I said.

I swear she almost giggled. "Okay." She read the text and grinned. "That was Dolly. Our special guest has agreed to come."

It wasn't long ago that my aunt and Dolly weren't on the best of terms. They were always competing for who ran the most successful restaurant, but they'd since mended that broken fence. I looked over at Jaxson to see if he knew anything about a sixth gossip queen, but he subtly shook his head.

"Are you going to share the name of this special guest?" Jaxson asked.

"It's Gertrude Poole."

Okay, I hadn't expected that. Gertrude was the town's psychic. She also had been training Rihanna to follow in her footsteps someday, and I had to say my cousin was an excellent student. Rihanna's ability to read minds was a bit unsettling, but thankfully, she'd been able to control when she listened and when she didn't. "That's awesome. You ladies will have a great time."

"I hope so." Our food arrived. "I'll leave you two to your meal. I'll see you, Glinda, tomorrow. And Jaxson, enjoy your family time."

"Thanks."

I dug into my food. "I am so happy Aunt Fern will be with friends this afternoon," I said once I stopped long enough to take a breath.

"I agree, and I'm equally as glad that we will be together as well. I can't wait for you to open the present I got you."

I'd always spent Christmas Eve with my parents, so being with Jaxson would be extra special. I was also glad my parents would have a quiet evening together for a change. "Can you give me a hint at what you got me?"

He chuckled. "Not on your life."

"Fine. Be that way." I tried to act offended, but I'm sure the smile on my face showed him I wasn't. For the rest of our meal, we talked about our usual issue of how to drum up new clients for our business. Witch's Cove was a small town, and it wasn't as if someone was murdered every day or every week for that matter. "We need to focus on investigating disappearing relatives, cheating spouses, and such," I said.

Jaxson chuckled. "You'd be bored within the year if that is

all we did."

He knew me too well. "I know, but unless we move to a city where there is more crime—which I would never do—that might be all we can do." It was probably why we were the only private investigation firm in town, and Witch's Cove couldn't even support us.

"We'll figure something out."

That was what he always said. When we finished, I tried to pay, but my aunt wouldn't hear of it. "Call it an early Christmas present."

I leaned across the counter and hugged her. "Thank you. You are the best. Have fun with the girls, and I'll see you tomorrow."

After I zipped up my jacket, we walked back to the office so I could pick up Iggy. I needed to head home in order to get ready for my hot date.

When we entered, Iggy was on my desk sniffing the mistletoe. "What are you doing?" I asked.

"I was wondering if I sprinkle some catnip on this stuff if it would work between me and Aimee."

Aimee was my aunt's cat who, by a mistake of magic, was given the ability to talk just like Iggy. Being a cat though, one moment she would pay attention to my familiar, and the next Aimee would ignore him. "Mistletoe is more for New Year's Eve than Christmas Eve, but to be honest, it can be used any time during the holiday season."

"Use it how?" he asked.

I certainly didn't mind a demonstration. Just as I picked it up, Rihanna came out of her room. "I thought I heard voices."

I was sure she heard more than just our voices. She'd

probably read my mind and came out to see the fireworks when I bestowed the toe-tingling kiss on Jaxson. Fine, I'd give her something to see.

I lifted the mistletoe over my head and walked over toward Jaxson. "Iggy wants to understand how this mistletoe works. Watch and learn, people."

I pulled Jaxson's head toward mine with my free hand. The second we kissed, my world spun, and then a bright light swirled around me. The intensity made me feel as if I were falling.

Then everything stopped, and the air was sucked out of the room. When I opened my eyes to see if maybe I'd fainted, what I saw totally and completely stunned me.

Chapter Two

I IMMEDIATELY CHECKED out my strange surroundings. Surely, I'd passed out and was now dreaming. It was the only plausible explanation.

"Glinda?" Jaxson said in a voice I barely recognized. I was thankful I could hear him after what had happened—whatever that was.

"I'm here." I would have sat up, but I was already standing and still holding the dang mistletoe over his head. I lowered my arm. "Where are we?"

"I don't know," Jaxson said.

All three of us looked around. Make that the four of us. Iggy was clinging to my leg. We were inside some large home that looked like a movie set from *Gone With The Wind*. In front of us sat a huge staircase that had statues of women on both newel posts. Yikes. The carpet and matching runner were red with ornate cream-colored designs running through them, and part of the ceiling looked like the Sistine Chapel. Oh, my. Being a former math teacher, I didn't excel in history, but I'd say this house might have been Victorian.

Only then did I notice we were all wearing heavy winter coats that I'd never seen before. Rihanna had on a blue puffy jacket, a red cap, and blue jeans that had really wide legs. She never wore anything but skinny jeans and black ones at that.

My cousin's mouth opened as she pointed to me. "Who are you? And where is the real Glinda Goodall?"

I thought she was kidding until I saw I was dressed in similar attire. I had on a long, black coat and blue jeans with wide legs too, only mine had a massive number of embroidered flowers on them. Never in a million years would I have worn something like that.

Thinking Jaxson might be a figment of my imagination, I reached out and touched him, but to my surprise, he was quite solid and not some ghost. How could that be? "Am I in a dream?" I whispered.

I don't know why I even asked, but that seemed the most likely explanation for what was going on.

Before he could answer, a tiny woman came out of a side room through a carved wooden archway that was a good twelve feet tall. "There you three are. How was your walk?"

My mouth went slack as my mind raced. Jaxson and I had just come from the Tiki Hut Grill, but I had a sinking feeling that wasn't what she was referring to. "Fine."

That answer seemed general enough not to raise any red flags.

The woman wove her hands together. "Wonderful. So, is there something I can help you with?"

Did she ask because we all looked lost? I glanced over at Jaxson. He always knew what to say in these awkward situations. I wasn't about to admit that I needed help figuring out where I was. She'd think I was crazy.

Jaxson cleared his throat. "I hope so. A few days ago, I was in an accident and my memory is rather jumbled. What is the name of this town again?"

I spotted a sign on a side desk that read, *The Ashton House B&B*. I'd never heard of it, and I certainly would have since I knew all of the places to stay in Witch's Cove.

"I am so sorry to hear that, young man. You're in Charlotte, Ohio."

Ohio? What kind of game was she playing? I wanted to laugh, but this woman appeared quite serious. A quick glance out the window told me we weren't in Florida anymore. Except for a few evergreens, the trees were devoid of leaves. It was almost as if we'd been transported into my mother's dream—that of being in the land of Oz—her all-time favorite movie.

An old car drove by that looked as if it got about ten miles to the gallon. Who drove something that big anymore?

I would have suggested we turn around and walk out the door, but from this woman's comment, we'd come from there. Did that mean we had rooms at this B&B? Out of instinct, I patted my pockets for a key. My plan was to say I'd forgotten it and ask if I could get another keycard, though from the looks of this place, they probably used skeleton keys.

I mentally snapped a finger. I bet Gertrude Poole did this. She probably thought it would be fun to put a spell on me, to make me think I'd gone back in time. I was totally convinced of that until the windows on this huge home rattled, confirming it couldn't be a dream of my own making. When I looked outside to see what caused the bluster, snow was falling. It was the first time I'd seen it in person, and I almost smiled.

"I can't find my key," my cousin said, clearly having read

my mind—or else she had noticed the panic sweeping across my face.

"I gave it to Glinda," the old lady said.

What? She knew my name? That was creepy, unless she was just a figment of my imagination, too. Not wanting to look like a fool in case any of this was real, I checked my pockets. Sure enough, I had a key. I lifted it out. "Here it is." A carved wooden number three was attached.

Jaxson made a show of sticking his hands in his pockets. His eyes grew wide as he lifted out another key with an attached number four. "Got mine."

He might have sounded cheerful to an outsider, but I could hear the confusion in his voice.

"Great," said the woman who I had to assume ran or else owned this B&B. "Breakfast is from seven to nine tomorrow morning. Since it's Christmas Day, most of the stores will be closed, so our cook will be serving Christmas Dinner at six sharp."

All of this was overwhelming, but as much as I wanted to ask what year it was, I didn't want her to think we had lost our minds. The bell bottoms I was wearing alone would imply this wasn't anywhere close to the twenty-first century. "Thanks."

I had no idea where rooms three and four were located, but if I had to hazard a guess, I'd say they were upstairs. I headed there, and Jaxson and Rihanna followed. Thankfully, Iggy had crawled under my coat. If the diminutive, gray-haired lady had seen him, no telling what she'd have done.

As soon as we were alone in the hallway, I faced them. "Do either of you know what's going on?"

"No," Jaxson said. "Let's convene in your room and see if we can figure it out."

I found room three and opened the door but stopped so quickly that Jaxson ran into my back.

"What's wrong?" he asked a second after he grabbed my shoulders to keep from knocking me over.

I stepped inside, my gaze trying to make sense of the gold framed photos, the large four poster bed, and the lavish setting. "Nothing is wrong, except that I've never seen any place like this before."

Rihanna walked around the room. "Look at this television. It must be a hundred years old."

Being a teenager, it didn't surprise me she'd focus on that item first. I didn't want to tell her that televisions weren't invented a hundred years ago. However, she wasn't too far off in guessing its age. The television was box-shaped and had a screen about the size of my laptop.

Jaxson said nothing as he toured the room. "Ah, Glinda, I think we have the wrong room. There are suitcases in here."

"But my key worked."

"Let me see about my room. Be right back."

While we waited for him to return, I checked out the attached bath and quickly decided it really needed to be updated. I did like the pink wall tiles, however.

"Come over here and look at this," Rihanna said.

I moved next to her. She was standing at a window that overlooked a residential street. The cars that were parked in the driveways were all the size of boats and quite vintage looking. "Maybe this town is famous for holding antique car shows."

"Maybe," she said.

Jaxson returned holding a newspaper. "Ladies, you have to see this."

"It's a paper. So?" I asked.

"You won't believe the date." He tapped the center line.

Rihanna and I leaned closer. "That's funny," I said. "December 24, 1972."

"I don't think it's meant to be funny. I, too, have a suitcase in my room that contains men's clothes my exact size. Not only that, but look at this." He showed me a wallet. Inside was a driver's license with his name and photo on it. "Notice the date of issue."

I read the Florida Driver's license information. "It says 1969. That's crazy."

"I know, but I can't explain it. See if you and Rihanna have something similar in your suitcases."

Now I was quite intrigued. One of the suitcases was pink and the other black, neither of which had wheels. The suitcase colors were a bit too coincidental, especially considering our fetish with wearing only one color. Naturally, I lifted the pink case and placed it on the bed so I could examine its contents. Rihanna did the same for her black one. We opened them up and looked through the clothes. The styles were definitely out-of-date.

Rihanna held up a pair of jeans to her five-foot ten-inch frame, and they seemed to be the right length. I did the same and then looked at the label. "They are size ten. That's a little small for me, but maybe they'll fit if I inhale. Who would go to all this trouble of buying us clothes, assuming they were meant for us?"

Jaxson walked over to the loveseat. "Two purses are on the floor." He picked them up and handed them to us.

They were made of cloth, designed to be worn over the shoulder. I looked inside and found a wallet, a checkbook, and a pouch of makeup.

Rihanna's contained relatively the same items. She opened her wallet. "Oh, my goodness. It's a really bad picture of me on my license."

"What town does it say you live in?" Jaxson asked.

"Jacksonville. How can that be?"

That was where Rihanna used to live. I read mine. "Witch's Cove, dated November 1966. What in the world is going on?"

"Do you think Gertrude had a hand in this?" Rihanna asked. "I certainly didn't put a spell on us."

"She probably has the ability to make us believe our surroundings have changed, but why would she?"

Iggy crawled up the wall to the window. "The glass is freezing. That is not my imagination."

"Don't look at me. I don't have the power to make people think they are in a different time and space. And if I could do this, I would never have brought you here. It's too cold for a lizard." I looked in my suitcase, and to my total surprise I found two outfits that I bet would fit him. I held them up. "Iggy, have you ever seen these before?"

He crawled down the wall and waddled over. "No, but I wouldn't mind another layer of clothes."

I dug deeper and pulled out what looked like a warming pad. I'd never owned anything like it, but the picture of an iguana on it implied what it was used for. "Let me plug this in and see if it helps."

I had no idea if any of this was real, but if it was, I didn't want Iggy to suffer. He hopped on the pad and waited for it to warm.

"It's working," he said a minute later.

"Good. Not that I really believe in it, but do any of you think it's possible we time traveled?" I kind of felt stupid even mentioning it since that was stuff I'd only read about in books.

Jaxson blew out a breath. "Until a few minutes ago, I'd say no, but I have no way to explain the clothes, the drivers' licenses, and the gear clearly meant for Iggy."

Rihanna rushed over to the television. "I'll see what's on the TV. That might give us a clue."

"Smart thinking."

Jaxson and I moved closer since the television screen was rather small. She looked around. "Any one see the remote?"

I spotted what I thought might be one, but it didn't look like the universal I was used to. "Just start pushing buttons to turn it on."

In no time, the TV burst to life. The clarity was terrible, but at least the shows were in color. She flipped through the channels and stopped at one. "Who is this Marcus Welby?" she asked. "That guy with him is cute."

I stepped closer. "I think that's a really young James Brolin. He's married to Barbara Streisand. I know this only because my mom always drooled when he starred in some Hallmark Channel show."

"I've heard of Streisand, but that's all," she said. Rihanna turned the channel again. "Here's another one."

"Wow," I said. "It's the Carol Burnett show. I've seen a few reruns. She's funny."

Rihanna continued to flip through the stations but soon returned to the beginning. I was starting to get the sinking feeling all of this might be actually happening. While this might be a fun adventure, I wished I had a clue how to get back to Witch's Cove in time for a warm, snowless Christmas with my family.

Chapter Three

AFTER COMING TO the conclusion that we were in some kind of time warp, we decided to check out the town for more clues regarding how we got there and maybe how we could return.

I also was hoping to find some food. Rihanna hadn't eaten lunch yet, and I didn't want to wait until tomorrow morning for my next meal.

Unfortunately, most places were closed, but we did find that the River Bend Café, a charming looking place in the middle of town, was open. Inside, only about three tables were taken. Considering it was cold and windy with an occasional snow flurry, I was surprised anyone was out and about—especially the day before Christmas. I was just happy we'd made it, since we had to walk almost a mile to get here, passing an interesting looking college and then traversing a rather slippery sidewalk downhill!

By the time we grabbed a booth and settled in, my nose and feet were seriously cold. Even though I was dressed in boots and had on gloves, it wasn't enough to keep me warm. Only macho Jaxson seemed unaffected. Good thing Iggy opted to stay back at the B&B. He would have frozen.

While it didn't look anything like Dolly's Spellbound

Diner, this one had a lot of charm. Black and white pictures of steamboats carrying coal down a river, along with some rather depressing images of coal miners, lined the wall.

A woman in her fifties, wearing a really cute pink uniform topped with a pink and white striped apron, approached. "Hello there. I'm Sissy. What brings you out on a blustery Christmas Eve?"

It was a natural question for anyone to ask. Most likely Sissy recognized us as newcomers and wanted to be friendly. I don't know why I didn't have an answer ready.

"I'm thinking about coming to school here in the fall," Rihanna said, clearly having read my mind once more. "It's about the only time I had to come. My cousin and her boyfriend volunteered to escort me." Rihanna tossed out a blazing smile. At that moment, I knew she must have inherited her father's ability to think on his feet.

Sissy's eyes sparkled. "How nice of you to bring her here. Where are you from?" she asked me.

"Florida," I said.

"Oh, my. This is a change I bet." She turned back to Rihanna. "What are you interested in studying?"

We all knew the answer, but it was possible Charlotte didn't offer a photojournalism major. "I haven't decided." Rihanna was smart not to be specific.

"You'll figure it out. I'm sure you came to eat and not chat with little old me. Here are the menus. I'll give you a few minutes to decide."

She dropped them off and left. "Great answers, Rihanna. We need to stick with that story." I looked back at Sissy who was wrong about one thing. I *was* there to chat. The time and place may have changed, but not my desire to solve a mystery.

Rihanna cleared her throat, and I returned my attention to her. "If I'm going to be a journalist, I need to be able to think on my feet," she said.

As a sleuth, I should have the same ability, but clearly, I did not. "You have that talent in spades."

I picked up the menu and checked it out. It looked like standard fare. It was nice to know something hadn't changed in fifty years. A hamburger and an iced tea sounded good to me, even though we'd just had lunch at the Tiki Hut—or so I believed.

When Sissy returned, she took our order. "I forgot to ask. Where are you all staying?"

I was glad I'd seen the name of the place. "The Ashton House B&B."

Her eyes slightly widened. "That is nice."

I hope not so nice that we couldn't afford to pay for it. "It looks like a fascinating place for sure."

"And so mysterious."

I sat up. The word *mystery* had my pulse beating a bit harder. "Why is that?"

"You don't know?"

If I had, I wouldn't have asked. "No. Do tell."

Sissy might be a bit worn around the edges from working so hard, but she still maintained an air of sweetness. How did I know? Just my gut feeling.

"The house used to belong to Richard Ashton. He was really, really rich. Kind of the Howard Hughes of Ohio."

That was rich.

"How did he make his money?" Jaxson asked.

"He invested in everything from the main hotel downtown, to cargo ships, coal, and a glass blowing company. Everyone in town liked him. He was very generous with his money until his wife died, and then he became a recluse. I heard he never left his house after that. Apparently, his two servants did everything for him."

I bet those servants could tell a tale or two. "What a shame. When did he die?"

She shrugged. "I think like thirty years ago." She leaned closer. "Rumor has it, he didn't believe in banks since the war was coming, so he invested in diamonds and gold."

"That was probably a smart move," I said. Both would have held their value even into our time.

"Everyone thinks he stored those diamonds somewhere in his house, though no one has ever found them, and trust me, Mrs. Tully has looked. As for the gold, rumor has it, he buried it all in the backyard."

Living in Florida, we'd heard more stories of sunken treasure than I care to recall, but I never knew of anyone who'd actually found any. I bet Mrs. Tully perpetuated the story to attract more house guests. I had to hand it to her. Maybe Aunt Fern should claim some famous person ate at the Tiki Hut and then buy a plaque to commemorate it. I inwardly chuckled. That was a bad idea. Mom would insist the famous person be Judy Garland who was Dorothy from *The Wizard of Oz*.

Sissy waved the paper with the order and smiled. "You'll never get your food if I don't turn this in."

As soon as she left, I opened my purse to make sure I could pay for the meal. I didn't have my money on me when

I'd kissed Jaxson, so why would I now? I'd tossed my purse on the sofa as soon as we'd walked into our office.

Aha! Inside this purse was a wallet with some cash and one credit card. It was a Diners Club card. Interesting. I hope they accepted it here. I had to wonder how much money I even had in my make-believe bank account, assuming whoever had arranged all of this thought that far in advance. Surely, they wouldn't want me to starve or have to find a soup kitchen.

I picked up the menu and did a mental estimate of how much it would cost.

"Have enough?" Jaxson asked, nodding to the open wallet.

"I think so."

"I know you think—or rather you wish—this is a dream, but I have to say, it feels all too real to me."

"Me, too," Rihanna chimed in.

"Fine. I'm going to proceed with the notion that this is real, which means we have to figure out how to get back home to Florida—and soon."

"You could put the mistletoe over Jaxson's head and kiss him again," Rihanna offered.

It made sense. I kissed him before and poof. We had been transported back almost fifty years. "It's worth a try."

Sissy carried over my tea, along with two hot coffees for Rihanna and Jaxson.

"Thanks. Could we get a piece of lettuce, too? I saw a stray cat outside the B&B and thought I'd feed her."

"Sure, but I could give you some scraps of chicken if you like."

A real cat would like chicken, but not Iggy. "Lettuce is fine."

"Okay, but I have three cats at home, and I'm not sure any one of them would touch the stuff."

I was sinking fast, but I decided just to smile.

Sissy nodded and then stepped over to another customer. "A cat?" Jaxson whispered.

"I don't think she'd believe me if I said I had an iguana."

Jaxson chuckled. "You might be right."

Everything about the diner, from the cash register on the counter to the way everyone was dressed, implied this was indeed the 1970's. If someone had transported us here, why Ohio and why this time period? Sure, I'd wished for snow, but why not Rockefeller Center in New York City? That town was about as iconic as one could get. I would have loved to watch the skaters and then shop at some of the big stores.

Ten minutes later, Sissy returned and delivered our food. "Enjoy. Let me know if you need anything else, food or information."

I smiled. Now there was a woman after my own heart—and she didn't even judge me to be too crazy. "Thanks."

We all dug into our meal, and Rihanna groaned. She had been hungry. After a few bites, she leaned back. "I'd give anything to have my camera with me. This would be a wonderful place to take pictures."

"I agree." I nodded to a portion of the river visible from the front window. "There aren't any boats on the water today, but I bet in the warmer months there must be some recreational vehicles. I can see myself sitting on the banks, soaking up the sun, and enjoying the tranquility of the flowing river."

"That would be nice," Rihanna said.

It was pure fantasy since I planned to be gone from here ASAP. As I was finishing my meal, I tried to think of other questions I could ask Sissy. I thought about seeing if there was a psychic in town, but at the moment I wasn't up for the reaction of distrust that often came when I asked about the occult. And I certainly wasn't about to say I was a witch who needed to talk to a fellow soul. If she asked me to prove it, I would be hard pressed. Rihanna might be able to read Sissy's mind, but that might scare the poor woman.

By the time we finished, it was getting dark, and I'd rather walk up the hill when I could still see.

After we asked for our check, I paid in cash. "I'm sure we'll be back," I said.

"Please do. Charlotte College is great. We have a wonderful town," Sissy said as she handed me something wrapped in aluminum foil. I had to assume it was the lettuce.

"Thanks."

Ready to brave the cold, I stepped outside. Brrr. I shivered because the temperature had dropped ten degrees just while we were eating. I was grateful that it had at least stopped snowing and that whatever had accumulated on the sidewalks was now gone.

All during the walk back, I couldn't help but wonder if the lore surrounding Richard Ashton was true. If he'd rarely left his house, what had he done with his wealth? I should have asked if he had any children. They might have a better idea what was true and what wasn't.

I shook my head. What was I thinking? My immediate goal was to unravel the mystery of how we arrived here and then to get out. I didn't need to worry about some eccentric old guy. And I certainly wasn't about to pull up floorboards looking for his hidden treasure.

Despite Jaxson's arm around my waist, it was darn cold. I might have been tempted to flag a cab, but I never saw one. Since cell phones didn't exist, it wasn't like we could call an Uber or anything. How did people survive in the 70's?

Eventually, we made it back. When we walked into the Ashton B&B, three men were in the main salon drinking coffee, and I was glad to see that Mrs. Tully had other guests. One of them was a mustached older man close to sixty, wearing a jacket with leather patches on the elbows. A professor perhaps? The other two could have been his sons, except they didn't look anything like him. One had bone white skin and sported long, light-colored hair to his shoulders, while the other was lanky with dark curly hair tied back and looked as if he had a healthy tan. I couldn't hear what they were saying since they were keeping their voices low. Had it been important, I would have had my cousin do her mind reading thing.

Jaxson gently clasped my arm and led me toward the stairs. He probably thought I was merely staring off into space, when in reality I was analyzing my surroundings.

He leaned close. "We don't need to attract attention."

"What was I doing?" I honestly had no idea.

"You were staring."

I nearly laughed. "There is no crime in that."

Rihanna came up behind us. "They're plotting something."

Aha! She had been reading their minds. This would be fun to find out what she learned. I waited until we'd reached the top of the stairs before I asked her. "What did you hear?"

Chapter Four

"I DIDN'T HEAR a whole lot," Rihanna said. "Just bits and pieces of words like *look* and *search*."

"Let's get into our room, ladies. We don't know if these walls have ears."

That was a terrible thought. Inside our room, I removed my jacket.

Iggy rushed up to us. "How was it out there?"

"Cold but interesting." I pulled the foil package from my purse and unwrapped it. "The nice lady at the café wanted you to have this." I placed it on the ground.

"Cool." Iggy dipped his head and munched on it.

While he was chowing down, I turned to Rihanna. "Did you get any other vibe off those guys?"

"Just that they were friends. I can't draw any conclusion off of two words."

"I understand."

"What about trying the mistletoe experiment?" Jaxson said. "Rihanna might be right. That kiss got us here. Maybe we can reverse it."

"I'm willing to try."

The mistletoe was on the table next to the sofa. I picked it up, or rather what was left of it. "What the heck?" My pulse actually soared as I spun toward Iggy. "What happened to this? Did you eat the mistletoe?"

"I was hungry, and I didn't know if you'd ever return."

That was totally lame. "We were just going out for a quick meal."

He lifted a leg as if to shrug and then puffed out his chest. "You already used it to get your kiss. I didn't know you could use it a second time. Like that wish coin. It was a one-time deal, you said."

"The coin, maybe, but not the mistletoe. Here's the thing. Mistletoe is poisonous."

"Not to me, it's not. I'm magical."

"Not all that magical." I picked him up and held him to my chest. "Are you sure you're okay? How is your breathing?"

"I'm fine. Put me down. You're embarrassing me."

He was fifteen. As a teenager, he wouldn't want to be seen coddled by his mother—if I could be so bold as to call myself that—especially in front of his idol, Jaxson, so I returned him to his heating pad.

"Let me know if you don't feel well."

"Maybe I should stay in Jaxson's room tonight," he said with too much cheer.

I stilled. I had the sneaking suspicion that he hadn't eaten the mistletoe but rather destroyed it, so I'd let him be with another man. "Fine, but take your heating pad with you."

Jaxson chuckled. "I got this. I won't let anything happen to Iggy. If I could get my hands on a computer, I'd do a little research on whether the plant is poisonous to animals."

I chuckled. "Even if you had a personal computer, which I don't believe had been invented as early as 1972, the

Internet wasn't around."

"This is the Stone Age. How did anyone get their information?" He held up a hand. "I know. They went to libraries or looked in Encyclopedias."

"I hadn't heard that word in forever." I checked the damaged plant again. At least the bow was intact. "Maybe when I'm not so upset about Iggy, we can try that kiss tomorrow using what's left of the mistletoe."

"I'd like that very much." Jaxson winked and then picked up Iggy and his gear. "I'll knock on your door somewhere between seven and nine for breakfast. Then we can figure out how to get back to our time."

"I like that plan."

Jaxson kissed me briefly. "Don't worry. We'll figure something out."

Famous last words.

SINCE I WASN'T all that tired, and the books that were in the room didn't interest me at the moment, Rihanna and I watched television. Unfortunately, the shows didn't hold much appeal either. It could have been because I knew my family would be beside themselves tomorrow when we didn't show up for Christmas.

At midnight, I wished Rihanna a merry Christmas and debated knocking on Jaxson's door to collect on that kiss, but I decided it was better to keep my focus on the here and now.

There was only one bed, so Rihanna and I had to share. My cousin might be tall, but she didn't take up much room.

In all honesty, I expected to be tossing and turning all night, but somehow, I managed to drop off into a dead sleep. I only roused because of some noise outside the room. I assumed someone from the restaurant below had come up the stairs to locate the Tiki Hut bathroom. It wasn't the first time that it had happened, and it wouldn't be the last, but why today of all days, when I was having a nice dream?

When no one knocked, I opened my eyes, and it took me a few seconds to realize I wasn't in my bed in Witch's Cove. The mattress moved next to me. What?

I looked over to find Rihanna stretching, and our serious time travel situation came flooding back.

She sat up, and her long, dark hair fell about her shoulders. "We really are here, aren't we?"

"I'm afraid so." I looked over at her. "Merry Christmas, by the way."

She huffed out a laugh. "Hardly merry. You know half of Witch's Cove will be out looking for us. I know Gavin will be pounding on Sheriff Rocker's door, demanding he find me."

"I know. Only they won't find us. How can they?"

"If it is a spell, maybe time has stood still."

I loved my cousin's optimism. "If we're making up cool scenarios, when we go downstairs for breakfast, there will be a ten-foot tall pile of money on the table with our name on it."

Rihanna chuckled. "That would be nice. What would you buy if you had a ton of money?"

Did Rihanna really expect an answer before I'd had my first cup of coffee? "I have no idea, but I'll get back to you on that." I pushed off the blankets and shivered. "First dibs on the shower."

She tossed off her sheets. "Hey, that's not fair."

"First come, first served," I said laughing as I rushed toward the bathroom.

"Don't take long. Breakfast is only served until nine, remember? And Jaxson will be here at any moment, though I honestly don't know what time it is." She held up her wrist. "Why couldn't they have had Apple watches fifty years ago?"

"Excellent question. While I take my very quick shower, how about knocking on Jaxson's door to make sure he's awake?"

"Can do."

I grabbed a change of clothes, grunted at my terrible non-pink options, and dashed into the bathroom. Instead of being a standalone, the shower was part of the bathtub. As long as the water was warm, I wouldn't complain.

While I waited for the water to heat, I brushed my teeth, happy to say whatever magical being had packed had done a good job. The toothbrush wasn't electric, but she'd managed to find my preferred brand of toothpaste.

Not being able to afford to dally, I hopped in the shower and washed quickly. I'd no sooner dried and dressed when Rihanna knocked on the door. "Jaxson is here."

I opened up. "Thanks. Be right out."

As soon as I stepped into the main room, Rihanna ducked in. "I'll only be a sec."

I presumed she needed to wash up a bit, too. Jaxson looked rather hip in his bellbottoms. "I like the long-sleeved forest green shirt. Is that in honor of Christmas since the tree in the lobby is a pine tree?"

"It is." He leaned over and kissed me. "Did you get any

brainstorms during the night about how we got here?"

"No. You?"

He shook his head. "I'm thinking we might need some help."

"I wish I knew where Gertrude grew up. I'd love to talk to the forty-year old Ms. Poole."

"That would be interesting. Or what about your grandmother? That conversation would be fun, I bet."

I smiled. "I would love that, but if I told her I was her granddaughter, she'd most likely laugh at me since she'd be about my age."

"Probably true."

"How is Iggy this morning?" I asked. "Any side effects from the poisonous berries or leaves?"

"Nope. I think Iggy is right. He might be immune to things like that."

"Something is up with him. He had to know that mistletoe was the last thing I was holding when we teleported—if that is the right word. Why would he destroy it?"

"When he's ready, he might tell you. There is a chance that he was hungry and didn't think about the consequences."

"Maybe."

The bathroom door opened, and Rihanna came out. "You look amazing in those jeans and that sweater," I said.

She spun around. "Maybe I'll stay here for good. I like the laid-back vibe of the area."

"That would be a hard no. If we ever figure out how we got here in the first place, when you turn twenty-one, you can return. Before then, you need to finish school."

Her brows rose. Instead of the smart aleck comeback I

expected, she just saluted and grinned, implying she was just teasing.

Downstairs, the two young men we'd seen chatting with the older man were sitting at a table eating breakfast. An attractive woman, who looked to be in her early fifties was sipping coffee and sitting by herself at a table for four. Her breakfast had not been served. Since I was a firm believer no one should eat alone, especially on Christmas, I thought we should join her. I looked at Rihanna, hoping she could read my mind.

My cousin nodded. "Let's ask if she is expecting anyone to join her."

"You are truly a remarkable, young lady," I said.

"Why, thank you."

The three of us stepped over to the woman's table. "Would you care for some company, or are you waiting for someone?" I asked.

She glanced up, swung her gaze toward Jaxson, and smiled. "By all means. I'm happy for the company. I'll be visiting my daughter and her family at two, but until then, I'm by myself."

I liked that she seemed the type to share, but I didn't like that she checked out Jaxson. Since I enjoyed connecting with people, I pushed aside my jealousy. We sat down, and when we introduced ourselves, I used Rihanna's reason for being in Charlotte.

"I went to college here, and I loved it."

I looked over at Rihanna. "Isn't that wonderful? You can ask her questions."

I didn't need to be a mind reader to know that my cousin

didn't like the pressure. Lying wasn't her style.

"Great." At least she smiled.

The woman pressed her lips together. "Excuse me. Where are my manners. I'm Stephanie Carlton."

"Glinda Goodall, and this is Rihanna Samuels, my cousin, along with Jaxson Harrison." I wanted to add he was my boyfriend, but maybe the less she knew the better. As much as I didn't want to discuss where we came from, I was too curious not to ask about her. "I guess if your daughter lives nearby, you've stayed here before?"

"A few times, yes. It is the nicest place in town, and Mrs. Tully is the sweetest lady."

Sissy had implied the same thing. "She runs this place all by herself?" I'd yet to see a maid or a man for that matter.

"Yes. Her husband died three years ago, and it's been tough for her. Work in the coal mines is sporadic, and if the men are out of work, then the businesses around here suffer, too."

"There aren't many tourists then?"

She smiled. "Not really. The college brings in a lot of the guests, especially around Homecoming, but with students out for the break, it's pretty desolate."

Then why were we sent here? Was there some higher power that wanted us to come to this town? If so, why?

Chapter Five

OUR BREAKFAST WAS outstandingly good, as was our chat with Stephanie. While she didn't provide much information that could possibly explain why Jaxson, Rihanna, and I had been sent to Ohio, I believed our purpose would be revealed at some point.

The discussion wasn't without some substance, however. We learned that the old man—the one who I thought looked like a professor—was indeed one. Turns out, Dr. Hamstead was doing a teacher swap with someone here at Charlotte College. That professor would in turn be moving to Louisiana to work at Hamstead's school: Embry-Tucker University.

Teaching someplace for a semester sounded kind of fun—especially if it was at the college level. The two young men with him were working on their PhDs. Stephanie wasn't really sure what they were studying, but she thought it had something to do with the business model of river traffic. That topic sounded really boring to me, but that might be why I didn't major in business.

By the time we finished our meal, it was past nine, which meant no other guests would be joining us—assuming there were others staying here. As we were about to leave, one of the young men called over to Mrs. Tully, who was clearing our plates.

"Yes? Can I get you something else?" she asked.

"No. We just wanted to know if Michael Hamstead already ate? He was supposed to meet us here at 8:30."

She shook her head. "I haven't seen him at all today."

The fairer of the two smiled. "Thank you."

With that interchange concluded, the three of us headed back upstairs. It was Christmas Day, so I doubted any shops would be open. That meant we'd have to be content to figure out why we were here and what to do about it by ourselves.

"Let me get Iggy," Jaxson said. "Be right back."

Iggy never liked to be left alone. I think that was why he ate the mistletoe—or perhaps destroyed it. He had a passive aggressive streak a mile long, something I hoped he'd grow out of soon.

Jaxson returned carrying Iggy. Some dogs looked guilty whenever they did something wrong, but Iggy had the best poker face. I never could read him. That meant he might have truly been hungry when he ate our potential path back to the present.

"Want to try the mistletoe again?" Jaxson asked.

"We have nothing to lose." Yes, it was mostly mangled, but it was worth a shot. Besides, I would enjoy kissing him.

I picked up my formerly lovely sprig and held it above our heads. I shouldn't be nervous, but I was. Why? Maybe it was because I feared this would fail, and we'd be stuck here forever.

Jaxson smiled. "Don't worry. It's just a kiss, pink lady."

Just a kiss. That's right. As soon as I closed my eyes, he leaned down. The moment his lips touched mine, warmth spread throughout me, as did a sense of security, but the air wasn't sucked from the room this time, and the lights didn't flicker like they had before.

When Jaxson broke the kiss, we both looked around. "We're still here," I said, trying not to sound too disappointed.

"I guess that wasn't the secret after all," he said.

"Or else I was too tense. Maybe we should try it again."

He grinned. "You won't get any argument from me. Let me hold it this time."

I had no problem with that. As soon as the broken sprig was over our heads, I stood on my toes and kissed him. I tried to ignore how pleasant it was and concentrate instead on being back in warm, sunny Witch's Cove. Never again would I complain about having balmy weather at holiday time. I even closed my eyes to mimic what we did before.

Jaxson sighed and leaned back. "It's different this time."

"I know. Maybe I'm too cold."

"I wish that were the problem, Glinda. I think the mistletoe is not the solution."

Darn. I wanted this to work. "Now what?" He shrugged. "And don't you dare say something will happen to give us a clue."

He laughed. "I'm just trying to be optimistic."

Right now, we needed more than a positive mind set. "We can't live here forever. We'll run out of money soon."

"We could rent a place and work," Rihanna said. "I don't think this area is very expensive."

"While true, jobs would only pay a fraction of what they do in our time."

"I don't think we need to worry about that yet, ladies."

Easy for him to say. "I hope so. In honor of it being Christmas day, is anyone up for a walk? The sun is out, and the wind looks very calm," I said.

Rihanna smiled. "I'm up for it. It's better than watching that old television."

I laughed. "Let me get my coat."

"Can I come?" Iggy asked.

"No. It's too cold."

"Then let me wander around the house."

Jaxson bent down and picked him up. "That's a no. Even dressed in clothes, someone would kidnap you since you're so cute."

"I'll cloak myself. Maybe I can find out some good gossip."

Iggy knew how to push my buttons. "Fine, but only if you promise to sneak into a room and then hide. You know you have a tendency to lose concentration and appear."

He did his circle dance of joy. "I promise."

"Okay but listen for our return and come back right away. Unless we find a shop that is open, I won't be staying out in the cold for long."

"Yes, ma'am."

Iggy never called me ma'am, but I didn't question him on it. This time, when Rihanna and I donned our gear, I did a better job of layering. Jaxson went next door to dress, too. When he returned, he said Iggy was safely roaming the halls.

I slung my purse over my shoulder, and we headed downstairs. "How about we go back to town?" I asked.

"Are you looking for something in particular?"

"No." Though if I found a psychic, I'd be happy. "Maybe they have some kind of occult store here. I'm sure everything will be closed today, but when they are open, someone might know of a spell to get us back."

"You think you can do a spell to time travel?" he asked.

"I was thinking I could try, but if it went wrong, we could end up in the middle of the Amazon jungle being eaten by bugs."

Rihanna laughed. "I guess the enemy you know is better than the enemy you don't know."

"Totally right."

This time, the trip to town seemed a lot shorter. Some snow was still perched on the bare limbs, and when combined with the evergreen trees and brilliant sunshine, it was pretty. Only now did I pay attention to all of the brick buildings that clearly belonged to the college.

"I wonder if they offer a photojournalism degree here?" Rihanna asked.

"If we're still here when the admissions office opens, we should ask." When my cousin's father died, he'd left her with enough money to last a long time. She could afford to go to a private school if she chose, but I wanted her to stay in Florida. Ohio was too far away.

"I'd like that."

We continued toward town. I was a bit disappointed that the River Bend Café was closed, but on the other hand, I was happy that Sissy wouldn't have to work today.

We passed a few chain stores that some time in the next fifty years would go out of business. Most here, however, seemed to be individually owned. A lot of artwork stores that included some combination of paintings, candle making, and glass blowing littered each street. Charlotte had a very homey feel to it.

"Glinda, look!" Rihanna said, as she pointed to a sign that led down an alley.

"Madam Criant's Psychic Readings," I read out loud. "Oooh, let's see where she's located. If she's for real, I'd love to talk to her in the next day or two."

"Let me lead," Jaxson said.

"Are you expecting someone to jump out of the alley and attack us?" I asked.

"Glinda, Glinda. Can't I be the protector for once?"

I hooked my arm around his and squeezed. "Of course. Please, lead the way."

The alleyway consisted mostly of backdoors that led to places such as restaurants, real estate offices, and art stores. One such sign read, Madam Criant's.

"Let's go around to the front," Rihanna said, acting quite animated.

Since I loved all adventure, I was definitely willing to check it out. When we reached the front, the inside was dark. I pressed my face to the window to look inside. A light flickered in the back and then a woman dressed in a long, flowing dress, and some kind of flowery turban came out from the back. She walked straight toward us and unlocked the door.

"Welcome. Please come in."

"Ah, we were just looking. It's Christmas, and I assumed you'd be closed."

"I'm open for you." She stepped to the side and motioned

us in.

I wasn't sure what to make of her cryptic message. She didn't know me, so she couldn't have been expecting us, or could she have? Once inside, I not only appreciated the warmth but the inviting atmosphere. Colored clothes hung on the walls, shell covered lamps dropped from the ceiling, and Persian rugs littered the floor. The strangest pieces of furniture were the beanbag chairs and the lava lamp.

"Please, have a seat."

How did she know we even wanted to stay? As if Rihanna thought the same thing, she grabbed my hand and led me over to the middle of the room. I slipped off my jacket and dropped down onto the chair. When it practically wrapped around me, I sighed. "This is great."

The woman smiled. "I'm glad you like it. I'm Madam Criant," she said.

"I'm Glinda, and this is Jaxson and Rihanna." I didn't see any need for last names.

"Let me get you some hot tea. It's rather cold outside."

I had no complaint about drinking something hot, but I thought it curious she'd assume we drank tea. "Sure."

As soon as Madame Criant stepped into the back, I looked over at Rihanna, hoping she'd been able to glean something from the mystery woman.

"She read my mind," Rihanna whispered. "She's the real deal."

"How could you tell? Did you read her mind, too?"

Rihanna nodded.

The curtains to the back parted, and our hostess returned with four steaming cups on a tray. She leaned over, allowing us to choose one. The really odd thing was that one tea cup was pink, another black, and the mug was green. The fourth was a delicate porcelain flowered cup that I bet was hers.

"Did you know my favorite color is pink?" I just had to ask.

The woman, who was about forty if I had to guess, shrugged. "I'm good at reading people."

Oh, my. Maybe Rihanna had allowed Madam Criant to learn about our preferences, but to have a pink cup in the back was a bit strange. I tasted the brew and sighed. "Perfect."

"I'm glad you like it. May I ask where you are from?"

As if she didn't know. I suppose it wouldn't matter if we told her the whole truth, and nothing but the truth, since we really did need to figure out how to get back to our time.

"We are from Witch's Cove, Florida."

Her eyes widened. "This is a big change."

"You have no idea."

Madam Criant sipped her tea. "Oh, I think I do. How are you finding the simplicity of life here?"

I stilled. She couldn't know we were from the future, could she? "It's refreshing."

I figured that would cover all answers.

"Tell me how I can help you."

I looked over at Jaxson. "Should we tell her?"

"I don't see why not."

I turned back to the psychic. "We're from the future, and we're trying to get back there."

"I know."

The old saying: You could have knocked me over with a feather certainly could have applied here. "You know?"

"I am a psychic."

Gertrude Poole was a psychic, and yet she didn't know a lot of things. Her knowledge usually came in the form of a vision. "Do you know what year we are from?"

"That's a bit harder to determine."

I slumped back in my beanbag. She didn't know. She was just trying to pretend she did. "Try 2020," I said.

"I bet it's a fascinating time." No surprise sounded in her voice.

"You don't know what it's like then?" Okay, that was uncalled for, but she'd gotten our hopes up.

"My knowledge is rather spotty, but I'm sure you are anxious to return there."

If she could help with that, all would be forgiven. "Most definitely."

"Well, that's easy."

Easy? She had to be kidding.

"What do we need to do?" Jaxson asked.

"Solve the murder."

I couldn't stop myself from laughing. For starters, we'd never mentioned we were sleuths, nor could she tell by the way we were dressed. "May I ask who died?"

"I suggest you return to your B&B and find out." Madam Criant stood.

We never told her we were staying at the B&B, though perhaps there weren't many choices in this small town. Once we placed our cups on the small table in front of us, I opened my purse to pay her. After all, she had provided the entertainment for the day.

"No payment is needed."

"Are you sure?" I asked.

"When you return, we will discuss it." With that, she picked up the tray and went back behind the curtain. It was almost like we'd just met the Wizard of Oz.

Chapter Six

WE HURRIED OUTSIDE and were met with a cold blast of air. "I really miss sunny Florida," I complained.

As much as I wanted to ask what they both thought of the strange interaction, I needed to get my thoughts in order first.

"She was telling the truth," Rihanna said without any prompting.

"Telling the truth about what?" I asked as I picked up the pace. I wasn't sure where I was going, other than to some place that was open and that served coffee.

"She believed we were from the future."

I was going to say something snarky about having an igloo in Florida I could sell her, but I kept my mouth shut. Madam Criant had been nothing but kind to us. She could have laughed in our faces, but she hadn't.

"I wouldn't have believed us either," Jaxson said.

"Neither would I," I chimed in. "The whole experience was unique. I had to say, she was a good sport to even open up for us. If we hadn't looked like frozen popsicles, I bet she wouldn't have asked us in."

"You're probably right," Jaxson said.

We were close to the river, and as such, had to walk the length of the town to get back to the hill that led to our B&B.

In that time, we didn't see any stores that were open, let alone ones that served food. "I guess we'll be begging for some hot coffee from Mrs. Tully."

"I'm good with that," Rihanna said.

Did I want to address the elephant in the room about the only way to get back to our life was to solve some yet to be determined murder? I did, but the big question was where to find someone who'd been killed?

By the time we climbed the hill to the B&B, my feet were tired, and my nose and even my eyes were cold. As we turned the corner to our street, I stopped dead in my tracks. "What the heck?"

Jaxson halted, too. "Why are there police cars in front of our B&B?"

I had to ask it. "Do either of you think someone was murdered here while we were gone?"

They both looked at me and answered at the same time. Only they didn't agree. Rihanna was looking very smug with her answer in the affirmative, whereas Jaxson was a definite no.

"Maybe we should head on in and ask," he said.

"Assuming they let us in," Rihanna added.

"They better, or they'll have another dead body on their hands—a frozen one."

Jaxson wrapped an arm around my waist. "Come on."

When we entered the foyer, quite a few people were in the sitting room. Both of the younger PhD students, Stephanie Carlton, Mrs. Tully, and a man I didn't recognize were there. The only one I didn't see was the professor.

A man in uniform approached. "I trust you three are

staying in rooms three and four?"

Mrs. Tully must have described us. "We are. What's going on?" I asked.

"I'm afraid Dr. Hamstead was murdered last night."

No. No. No. It wasn't that I was a stranger to murder. Far from it. Except for a brief glimpse of the man as I'd passed by the sitting room, I didn't even know him. The fact Madam Criant told us about the murder before we knew about it was really freaking me out right now.

"How did he die?" I managed to choke out.

"Ma'am, would you and your group please join the others in the sitting room? We're talking to each person individually."

The fact he didn't answer me was telling. Not wanting to cause any trouble, we moved to the room and found three seats together.

Rihanna lifted her chin. "Told you."

"Told us what? That Madam Criant is the real deal?" She nodded. I had to admit, she might be. "I know she said the only way to get back home was to solve this murder, but how can we do that? We don't know the sheriff, we have no gossip queens to help, and most importantly, we don't even have a computer to do research!" I was whisper-shouting, if that was even a word.

"We'll have to do it the old-fashioned way," she said.

"What's that? Tap our red shoes together three times and announce we want to go home?" I looked over at Jaxson who was almost smiling.

"We help solve it with legwork," he said. "And don't forget we have our ace in the hole."

"I forgot about Iggy. I can't wait to hear what he knows. I bet he'll be happier than a pig in the mud these next few days knowing there's a murder to solve."

Jaxson almost let a laugh out until he glanced behind me and stilled.

"Ms. Goodall?" announced a man who clearly was standing right behind me.

I twisted around. "Yes?"

"The sheriff would like to speak with you now."

Since I hadn't killed anyone, I was happy to learn what he had to say. "Of course."

I followed him to a small sitting room that contained a sofa, two chairs, a coffee table, and a television. On the wall was a board with pegs holding a few room keys. This must be where Mrs. Tully stayed during the day.

He motioned I take a seat. "Please state your name and home address for the record."

I didn't see any tape recorder, but who was I to question his methods? "Glinda Goodall." I rattled off my address.

"From Florida, you say?"

"Yes."

"What brings you to Charlotte?"

Excellent question. Telling him we were teleported here by witchcraft would have made me look like a suspect or someone who was quite deranged. Since I didn't want him to think either was true, I explained about Rihanna wanting to scope out the college here. When he didn't react, I figure I'd passed the test. "I heard the murdered man was Dr. Hamstead."

"That's correct," the very strait-laced sheriff responded.

"How did he die?" I assumed he'd tell me it was confidential.

"Someone struck him with a serving tray to the back of the head."

"That must have been one heavy tray," I mumbled.

"Why do you say that?" he asked with another deadpan response.

I guess it wouldn't do any harm to admit that my parents ran a funeral home, and that I was familiar with murder. "When I'm not waitressing at my aunt's restaurant, I help my mother prepare bodies for their mortuary. We are quite close with the medical examiner, and I've learned a lot. I don't think I've ever seen anyone die due to a blow from a serving tray."

"Is that so? Tell me, Ms. Goodall, how do you think Dr. Hamstead died?"

Out of habit, I reached up to touch the pink stone around my neck, only to find it wasn't there, and a slice of panic shot through me. I couldn't remember the last time I wasn't wearing the gift from my grandmother. "If I could see the body, I might hazard a guess." I don't know why I said that. I was useless without my magic stone.

"I'm afraid that is out of the question."

For now, I'd let it be. I never got very far with our sheriff either. One of the guests might have killed him or known something about it. With a little ingenuity, I probably could figure it out. "Okay. Do you have any idea when he died?"

"No. That's what medical examiners are for."

Funny man. He then asked whether I knew the professor. When I explained that we'd only arrived yesterday, I figured he wouldn't put me high on the suspect list.

"Thank you for your help," he said. "My deputy will be taking your fingerprints in order to rule you out as a suspect."

That was just an excuse, but I was okay with it. "No problem. Are we done here?"

"For now, yes, but please send in your gentleman friend."

I didn't know what Jaxson could add, but I doubt he'd be a suspect either. I was hoping Rihanna could do her mind stuff and learn something valuable.

After we had been fingerprinted, they called in Rihanna. It was rather nerve-racking to have to wait. I leaned over to Jaxson. "Do you think someone in this room is the murderer?"

His eyes widened. "I would know that how?"

"I know you wouldn't know, but maybe the sheriff let something slip."

He shook his head. "The guy was totally professional."

"I got the same feeling."

It wasn't long before Rihanna returned from her interrogation. Her slight smirk implied she'd learned something, though it wouldn't be smart of her to say anything since we didn't need the real killer to suspect we had a clue.

My cousin sat down. "When do you think we can go back to our rooms?" she asked.

I looked around, but I wasn't sure who had or who hadn't been interviewed. Rihanna's question was answered a few minutes later when the sheriff emerged from the room across the way. "I wish I could give you some information, but I don't know much. We are asking that if you must leave the B&B to let one of our officers know your destination. Until this investigation is complete, all of you need to remain in town. I'm sorry for the inconvenience. Oh, yes, and Merry Christmas."

Merry Christmas? Really? Did he suspect someone in the room or not? If I'd been the murderer, I'd say I was going out for dinner and never return. Right now, I could hope his team was fast, though if Madam Criant was to be believed, the four of us would be instrumental in bringing this case to a close.

Once we were dismissed, we hustled upstairs where we all piled into Rihanna's and my room. I spun around. "We should wait for Iggy. I bet he has some information."

"Let's hope so." Jaxson held up his hands. "I need to wash."

One by one, we cleaned up. I learned firsthand how hard fingerprint powder was to get off the fingers.

Once I finished, I cracked open the door so that Iggy could come in. Surely, he'd heard us clomp up the stairs, though it was always possible he was trapped in a room. If that was the case, he'd be mad when he finally got out. Several doors opened and then shut. Less than a minute later, tiny scratches sounded on our wooden floor.

"You in here?" I whispered.

"Yes," Iggy said. He reappeared and spun to face me.

I shut the door and blew out a breath. "Sorry that took so long for us to get back here," I said. "The sheriff made us stay downstairs while he interrogated each of us."

"I know. I was in that room."

"You were? Why didn't you say something?" I asked.

"I didn't know if any one of them was a witch or rather a warlock."

I chuckled. "Really? The sheriff was such a stick in the mud."

"Iggy's right," Jaxson said. "We don't know who is capable of understanding him. Iggy was wise to be cautious."

"I guess I'm used to being in Witch's Cove where I know who does and who doesn't have magic." I turned back to Iggy. "What did you learn?"

He waddled over to his heating pad. Thankfully, Iggy was capable of pushing the button to turn it on. Once situated, he faced us. "I didn't get all that much, but I did see the crime scene."

"Great. Tell us." I moved next to Jaxson, who was sitting on the loveseat, while Rihanna took the chair across from us so that Iggy wouldn't have to keep turning around to talk to each of us.

"The place was a mess. The guy was face down on the floor next to two broken tea cups."

"Two?" He nodded. "That implies someone else was there, though we don't know if it was the killer or not."

"Did they test the contents for poison?" Jaxson asked my familiar.

"I don't know. All I can say is that the medical examiner is there now," Iggy said.

"Did you see a serving tray?" I asked.

"Yes. I went over and checked it out. There was a dent in the thin metal, but I didn't see any blood on it."

My mind spun. "I realize you are not a medical professional, nor are we, but if there was no blood, did it look like that was what killed him?"

Iggy's mouth open and then closed. "Even if I'd been in

the room and witnessed the murder, I might not know what killed him."

"That's probably true."

"Maybe he had tea with someone, experienced a heart attack, and keeled over," Rihanna offered.

I pointed a finger at her. "Excellent point. How did the sheriff know he was even murdered? Who's to say that tray wasn't dented beforehand? Unless he saw a bullet hole in the man's forehead, he really shouldn't have jumped to the conclusion the man was murdered." I returned my attention back to Iggy. "Did you learn who'd called in the man's death?"

"No."

I looked at my other two colleagues. "That might be the place to start."

Chapter Seven

"IF WE'RE GOING to help crack this case, how about we divide and conquer?" Jaxson suggested.

That was smart. "Rihanna, why don't you talk to Mrs. Tully? I'm betting, she'll look at you like a granddaughter."

"What reason will I give for asking about the murder?"

That was a good question. "Tell her that you're really upset or something."

She shook her head. "I can't fake it that much."

"Okay, then ask her if she knows when Dr. Hamstead died. You thought you heard a noise in the middle of the night. If the sheriff's department told anyone what happened, it would be the B&B owner."

"I doubt it, but I can ask. What about you guys?"

"I know what Glinda is going to say, so I'll volunteer to speak with Stephanie." Jaxson winked.

I needed to defend my response. "She was checking you out."

"If you say so. And you?"

"I'll offer my condolences to the two PhD guys who came here to be with Dr. Hamstead. I bet they know something."

"That sounds great, but we really need to be careful," Jaxson said. "While it's totally possible some outsider came in and murdered Dr. Hamstead, it's more likely that one of the guests did it."

"I understand very well about the dangers of talking to murderers. Maybe we should list who our top suspects are before we rush into this?" I looked around, but no one said anything. That wasn't good. "Fine. I don't have a top suspect yet either since I know nothing about any of the guests. Can we at least make a list of who is staying in the house? And that includes maids, cooks, and maybe even gardeners."

"I doubt Mrs. Tully has a gardener in the winter," Jaxson said.

"Smart aleck." He was probably right.

"How about instead of looking like snoops, we see what happens during dinner?" Rihanna suggested. "I wouldn't be surprised if Mrs. Tully pushes all of the tables into one long configuration since it is Christmas. We'd be able to hear what others are saying and then ask them questions without anyone becoming suspicious."

I smiled. "That's an excellent idea. I'll speak to Mrs. Tully about the table arrangement in case she hasn't thought of it."

Jaxson stood. "If we're going with Rihanna's idea, I need to take a shower so I don't offend Ms. Carlton."

"I'll do the same," Rihanna said, "since someone hogged the shower this morning."

I just laughed. "Enjoy, but don't take too long. I can't vouch for how much water this old place has."

We discussed the possibility of Rihanna and I snagging seats at the table first. That way, if Jaxson came in later, he could choose a seat closer to Stephanie Carlton.

Jaxson tapped two fingers to his forehead. "Ladies, I'll see you two a little after six."

I half expected Iggy to follow him, but when he didn't, I suspected my familiar didn't want to leave his heating pad. It would be nice if he could come to dinner though. I knelt in front of him.

"Ooh, I feel like a king," he said.

"I'm down on my knees only because I didn't want you to get off your heating pad."

"Thank you."

"Assuming you can keep a low profile—which means hiding under the table—would you like to come to dinner tonight and spy?"

I assumed he'd jump at the chance. "What do I get for it?"

"Iggy, don't play this game. I know you're dying to be in the thick of things. Either you want to come or you don't."

He turned his eyes to the side. "Only kidding. Yes, I'll come."

"That's better." I stood. "I need to check with Mrs. Tully about the table arrangement. I'll be back in a jiffy."

As I headed toward the stairs, I passed the door to room six, which was open. Naturally, I couldn't help but look inside. Two crime scene investigators were in there, probably dusting for prints. Good luck with that. I had no idea how, or if, they could tell how long the prints had been there, but I bet the place had a ton. Right now though, my concern was making sure The Pink Iguana Sleuths were on the case.

Thankfully, Mrs. Tully loved the idea of having all of the guests seated together. She said that after the cook, Evan Drugan, finished preparing the meal in the kitchen, he'd be joining us, along with two other guests.

"That is so sweet of you to invite him."

"He is as much of the B&B family as any guest."

With my assignment completed, I went back upstairs. Rihanna and I would be going downstairs early in order to grab two seats next to each other in the middle of the table. That way, we might have better access to everyone. As we had discussed, Jaxson would come in later and take whatever seat was available. Hopefully, it would be close to where Stephanie sat.

When it neared dinner time, Rihanna and I went into the dining room. Yes! We were the first to arrive. Three seats—two on one end and one on the other—had a card labeled reserved. Those must be for Evan and Mrs. Tully's two friends. Next to arrive were the two students who were about my age, so I thought striking up some kind of conversation with them would seem natural. While I'd only taught middle school for a year, it might imply I was interested in academics.

"Please sit across from us," I said just as they were headed to the other end of the table. I wasn't one to flirt to get information, but if I had to, I would.

They glanced at each other. I couldn't tell if they needed permission from the other or if they had something to hide.

The fair-haired boy smiled. "Thanks."

Once they were seated, I introduced myself and Rihanna. Interestingly enough, the darker hair man focused on Rihanna while the pale-faced one studied me. He almost made me feel like a specimen in a museum.

"I'm Phil Fernandez, and this is my friend, Dominic Geno," said the lighter of the two.

We all shook hands. "I'm sorry for your loss," I said.

"Thanks."

"Will you be returning to...?" I didn't want to let on I knew where they were from.

"Louisiana? We haven't decided. We came to help Dr. Hamstead with his research, but now, our future is obviously uncertain."

"I can understand that." Iggy climbed down my leg, and I almost jumped at the unexpected movement. I was happy he was on the move, however. His hearing was excellent, his desire for gossip equal only to mine, but his ability to remember all of the details was often not the best. "Did I hear he was a history professor?"

"For the most part. He studied the history of transportation across America. More specifically, he was interested in the effects of river traffic on an area."

How terribly boring. I shouldn't talk, though. Most found math to be the same way. "What is your thesis about?"

While I didn't really care, I wanted to show them I was just some innocent nerd who asked a lot of questions.

Dominic nodded, acting as if he'd answer first. "I'm actually doing a feasibility study of the water flow of the Ohio River. I'm interested in learning about the possibility of creating an underwater turbine to create electricity to the area, whereas Phil is working on better use of the water for cooling the coal power plants."

I sat up. Now I was interested. "You're kind of physicists

then?"

A small smile came to his lips. "In a way. It's very boring scientific stuff."

"Nonsense. I'm interested." I actually was. I hadn't been challenged in this way in a while. "Tell me more."

"Ah... It's a fluid dynamics problem that requires us to work on the college's mainframe. We're working with the faculty to make our calculations and iterate the software as we apply it to see its limitations."

He sounded like he'd memorized a speech. But hey, maybe he had, especially if enough people asked him about it.

That was quite impressive, especially considering the fifty years of scientific advancement since then. "What programming language are you using?"

Dominic glanced over at Phil and then back at me. "Fortran."

"Is it a numerical analysis problem, or do you have an equation for an exact solution?"

The fear that crossed their faces had me taking notice. "The first one," Dominic said.

I'd bet anything they were frauds. The big question was how to prove it?

Phil tossed back his water. "Are you a math professor?" he asked.

"Just a math teacher." I decided to tell a little lie. I explained that I taught middle school math. The last thing I needed was for them to learn Jaxson and I were amateur sleuths who needed to find out who'd killed their friend.

Just then Jaxson arrived, which gave these two men the needed break—or so I assumed. My partner made a show of walking around the table and sitting across from Stephanie who'd arrived a bit ago, which had been our plan all along. Thankfully, the seat next to me had a *reserved* sign on it.

"I can switch seats with your friend if you'd like to sit across from him," Phil said.

"We're good. Since the start of this trip, we've seen too much of each other." I rolled my eyes for effect. "He's my best friend's brother. Drake would have come to help Rihanna check out Charlotte College, but he had work to take care of."

I hoped Jaxson couldn't hear me say any of that, because none of it was true.

Mrs. Tully came out, along with an exotic looking gentleman who appeared to be about forty. Both were carrying trays of salad, which couldn't have arrived too soon. I was starving.

They'd just served us when the front door opened and a woman in her mid-sixties came in, bundled up from head to toe.

"Oh, I see I am late. I am so sorry." She shrugged off her coat.

Mrs. Tully came over to her. "Don't worry. I saved you a seat. I'm glad you could make it."

"Me, too. I need to buy new boots. It can get slippery out there."

She'd walked there?

Mrs. Tully faced us. "Everyone, say hi to Sheila Lawson. She's our local librarian and a good friend of mine. We met at a grief meeting three years ago."

How sad and yet how wonderful to find a connection in such a painful time of her life. Mrs. Tully led her friend to the empty seat next to Jaxson. Mrs. Tully then sat at the head of the table so that they were sitting kitty-corner from each other.

Two seats remained. I figured one would be where Evan, the cook, would sit, but I had no idea who the remaining seat was for. After Mrs. Tully said the blessing, the conversation quieted as we gobbled down the salad. I know Iggy would have liked a piece of lettuce, but I wasn't sure how to get it to him without attracting attention. Perhaps tonight, I could sneak down into the kitchen and find something for him to munch on. He'd have been okay with green leaves, but in the winter, those were far and few between.

Halfway through the main course, my body buzzed a second before the front door opened. We all turned around—or at least I did. Never in a million years did I expect to see Madam Criant walk in. What in the world was she doing here? I certainly hoped she hadn't come to out us, though I sincerely doubt anyone here would believe we were from the future.

Chapter Eight

AFTER SWEEPING OFF her cape in a rather dramatic fashion, Madam Criant slipped into the seat next to me and grabbed hold of the cook's hand. "I apologize for being late, Evan."

He smiled at her with much affection. "We've only just begun. Let me fix you a plate."

Before I could ask what she was doing there, Madam Criant turned to me and held out her hand. "I'm Bethany Criant. Evan invited me to join him for the Christmas celebration."

Bethany? If she wanted to pretend we didn't know each other, I was okay with that. Perhaps she really did need our assistance in solving Michael Hamstead's murder and didn't want to let on that she'd asked us to help.

I introduced myself and then commented how cool it was that she knew Evan.

"Oh, we go way back."

That sounded rather cryptic, but I was kind of glad she was here. Madam Criant might be able to provide us with some insight as to who could be guilty of murder, especially if she was a good friend of the cook.

Wait! Is that how she knew Dr. Hamstead had died before we found out? It made total sense. Evan had probably called her right after the body was discovered. A bit relieved I'd figured that out, I sipped my glass of holiday cheer.

Evan returned with her meal and placed it in front of her. Once he sat down, he leaned over to Bethany. That name so didn't fit her. I would have gone with Cassandra or Evangelina—something more befitting the occult.

Evan clasped *Bethany's* hand. "I'm so glad you could come. I know you are busy."

"Never too busy to see you." Madam Criant smiled with deep affection.

As much as I wanted to get to know this enigmatic woman, it might be best if I pretended not to be interested in socializing with her. Because the two PhD students were sitting across the table, the five of us interacted, but I didn't really learn anything from the conversation. Unfortunately, with everyone talking, I couldn't hear much of what Jaxson was saying to Stephanie either, or what anyone else was talking about for that matter. I'd have to be content to wait until after dinner to have more intimate conversations.

I'd shared every Christmas with my family and missed them now more than ever. I couldn't help but wonder why Stephanie wasn't with her family. I didn't remember the sheriff insisting that we stay at the B&B at night. Interesting. Did she have a hand in Hamstead's death and wanted to make sure no one pointed the finger in her direction?

After the last case we'd solved, over Halloween, more than one person might be involved in the murder.

Once everyone finished, Evan and Mrs. Tully cleared the table and then served a chocolate torte. Evan definitely had mad kitchen skills. After the very rich dessert, we stood to stretch and mingle. The two young men excused themselves and retired upstairs before I was able to talk with them further. Darn. I sidled over to Jaxson, who was talking to Stephanie.

"We didn't get a chance to chat over dinner. It was a bit noisy," I said.

She smiled. "I know, but Jaxson kept me busy."

I hope he'd learned a lot. "I thought you'd be with your family."

Her shoulders sagged. "My granddaughter took kill—I mean, took ill—and my daughter thought it would be better if I kept my distance for a day or two."

"That makes total sense." What I wouldn't give to have the Internet so Jaxson could find out about her family. And no, that slip of the tongue did not go unnoticed.

When I glanced up to find Rihanna, she was following Mrs. Tully and carrying some dishes back to the kitchen. I had to hand it to my cousin. She was taking her assignment seriously.

Speaking of taking their job seriously, I bet Iggy had been working hard. Wanting to gather him, I pretended to look for my key.

"Lose something?" Jaxson asked.

"I think my key fell out of my pocket." I went over to the table and looked underneath. Sure enough, Iggy was there. I set my purse on the floor and motioned for him to climb in, which he readily did. For once, he didn't say anything. I think even he understood that Madam Criant probably could understand him.

I pulled out my key, stood up, and waved it. "Got it," I said as I walked over to Jaxson. "I'm going to thank Mrs. Tully and then head on upstairs." I turned to Stephanie. "I hope your granddaughter is feeling better soon."

"Thank you."

I went to the kitchen and found Rihanna washing the pots and pans. Mrs. Tully stood next to her, drying them as fast as she could and chatting away. I wanted to tell Rihanna how proud I was of her, but I needed to wait until we were alone before I did.

I placed a hand on Mrs. Tully's back to get her attention. "I wanted to thank you for the dinner. It was amazing."

Her bottom lip trembled. "I can't tell you how wonderful it was to have so many people here on this very special day. It's been so lonely since Arnie passed away."

"I imagine it has been. I'm going to retire for the evening." I turned to Rihanna. "I'll see you upstairs."

"I won't be long."

I went upstairs, anxiously wanting to find out what everyone had learned. As soon as I stepped in the room, Iggy crawled out of my purse. "It was cold down there."

"I'm sorry." He headed over to the heating pad. "I hope you learned something."

"I guess that depends on what Rihanna and Jaxson found out."

What about my information? It didn't matter. I was pleased he was being oddly mature about it all. A knock sounded on the door, and then Jaxson stepped inside. He walked over and hugged me.

"What was that for?" I asked.

"Can't I hug you on Christmas?"

"You can hug me any time you want."

He smiled. "Where's Rihanna?"

"Still in the kitchen. She must be learning a lot. Washing dishes isn't her favorite chore. What about you?"

"Stephanie let something slip, but I'll wait until Rihanna is here before we all share."

"Sounds good," I said. I looked around for a mini fridge only to realize they might not have had such amenities in old homes fifty years ago.

The room door open, and Rihanna came in. "Phew, what a night."

"Sit down and tell us about it." Since I wanted Iggy to feel included, I moved his pad from near the bed to the sitting area. "Who wants to start?"

"I will," Jaxson said. "About the only useful tidbit I learned from Stephanie was that her financial situation is a bit precarious."

"Then why is she staying in such a nice place?" I asked.

"She's been coming here for years."

"Did you check out her jewelry?" I asked.

"Not my thing."

I could believe that. "She's very well put together, and that look doesn't come cheap."

"I wouldn't know," he said.

"Did she ever say if she was divorced or married?" I asked.

"Widowed. The last husband ran through all his money and left her without much."

"That would be tough."

"Here's the part that's interesting. Stephanie was a little

vague about things, but it would seem as if she's been married three times. And get this. All three of her husbands have died."

I whistled. "Is she some kind of black widow?"

"I didn't get that sense." He turned to Rihanna. "Want to add anything?"

"Just that when the cook came out from the kitchen, she was giving him the eye but then seemed to dismiss him."

"Are you thinking she's looking for husband number four?" I asked.

"It's definitely possible," Jaxson said. "She pummeled me about my financial abilities."

"And?"

"I told her I was a stock boy, which instantly got her off my back."

"You are the farthest thing from a stock boy, but that will make a good cover if you want her to stay away."

"I do. Want her to stay away, that is. I'm not interested."

"Good."

Jaxson looked over at Rihanna. "You were sitting next to her. Did you get anything off her?"

"She was hiding something. I could tell she knew the deceased, but how well, I couldn't say."

"Knew him in what way?" Jaxson asked.

"As friends? Or maybe she thought he'd make do as husband number four."

I huffed out a laugh. "That almost implies she didn't kill him. She would have waited until she married him first."

We all enjoyed that one.

"What did you learn, Glinda?" Jaxson asked.

"Two things. One is that I don't think Dr. Hamstead's assistants are who they say they are."

"Why do you think that?" he asked.

I explained about Dominic's description of his thesis. "Something seemed off to me."

"Maybe it's because you know about modern day technology, or the poor guy could have just been nervous talking to a pretty girl."

He thought I was pretty? Jaxson was the best. "Maybe."

"What was the second thing?"

"When Madam Criant came in, she pretended as if she didn't know me."

"I bet she didn't want you to mention she was a psychic," Rihanna said.

"Why not?"

"People would ask too many questions."

"You might be right. Did you learn anything from Mrs. Tully?"

She shook her head. "Not much. She seems afraid of something, and that fear was blocking her thoughts from me."

"That doesn't help us." I turned to Iggy. "And you, my fine man, what did you learn?"

"Kind of what you guys already figured out, except that Dr. Hamstead was a thief."

"A thief?" My mind shot to the lore of the hidden diamonds. "What did they find in his room?"

"He'd taken a bottle of rum from the pantry. The sheriff questioned the cook, and he said he keeps very careful count of all the bottles."

"Maybe he told Mrs. Tully to put the bottle on his bill."

"Maybe," Iggy said.

I leaned back against the sofa and blew out a breath. "It doesn't seem like anyone is an obvious suspect. Any suggestions what our next step should be?"

"You gave me an idea," Jaxson said.

"Really? What?"

"What if Dr. Hamstead was a thief, and I don't mean just stealing liquor?"

"A diamond thief?" Iggy said. He did a circle dance.

"If he was, wouldn't the sheriff's department have found the diamonds already?"

Jaxson shrugged. "Who's to say they haven't?"

"I would have thought they would have said something."

"The sheriff seemed to be a very by-the-book kind of guy," Jaxson said.

"It's possible then that Dr. Hamstead hid them after he discovered their location. Regardless, I think we should do a bit more research on Richard Ashton."

"Didn't you forget we don't have Internet?" Rihanna tossed in.

"Then we'll have to go to the library," Jaxson said. "I bet Sheila Lawson can help us. I was sitting next to her, listening with one ear, and like all librarians I've met, she seems like the helpful type."

"I love the idea."

"I don't know when the University staff will return to work, but when they do, maybe we can talk to the admissions department about all three men," Rihanna said.

"Why?" I asked.

"If you got a gut feeling that these two students weren't

on the up-and-up, maybe Dr. Hamstead wasn't either. We should ask if he really had a job lined up at Charlotte College."

I stared at Rihanna for a moment, marveling at her. "You must have inherited quite a few of your brains from your father. That is brilliant."

She grinned. "Only brilliant if it turns out the guy was a fake."

We all laughed. "Tomorrow, we'll visit the library. Hopefully, it will be open and not too far from town."

"Maybe we can see if Madam Criant is free," Rihanna said. "I'd love to have her take on things."

"Me, too."

"If the River Bend Café is open, we might want to see what Sissy has to say," Jaxson said.

"Excellent suggestion. Our day seems to be full, so I think I will call it a night," I said.

Jaxson looked over at Iggy. "What's your pleasure, buddy. Want to see if we can scrounge up some food in the kitchen for you?"

"Yes, but can we take my heating pad?"

He laughed. "You bet."

I feared Iggy liked being with Jaxson more than me. If he didn't care for my familiar so much, I might have complained.

Chapter Nine

AFTER GETTING DIRECTIONS to the library from Mrs. Tully, and learning it was open for half a day today, the three of us took off. Iggy promised that he'd hide under the bed should a maid come in to clean the room.

"Do you think Sheila Lawson will be willing to talk about Richard Ashton?" I asked as we walked down the hill to the main town.

"Why wouldn't she be? If she's such good friends with Mrs. Tully, I bet she knows a lot," Jaxson said.

"You're right. She might even remember the guy."

"What are you hoping to learn?" Rihanna asked.

That was a good question. "I often don't know what I'm looking for until I find it."

She chuckled. "How does that usually work for you?"

"Surprisingly well, thank you." My methods might seem strange to many, but in the end, Jaxson and I often helped solve the crime. "You know, it just occurred to me that Madam Criant might not really have the ability to help us get home."

My stomach almost cramped at that horrible thought. I never should have said that—or even thought it for that matter.

"She said if we solved the crime, she'd give us the clue," Rihanna said. "Maybe she can't send us directly, but if she can point us in the right direction, it could do the trick."

"I hope you're right."

"You don't sound convinced. What are you thinking?" Jaxson asked.

"Madam Criant might have told us what we wanted to hear since we mentioned we were from the future and that we wanted to return. I'm betting there is a reason she wants us to be involved in trying to solve the murder." Or was I just really cold and scared that we'd never return home, and my mind was playing tricks on me?

"She seemed friendly with the cook," Rihanna said. "That was genuine."

"Yes, but I wonder what he knows. I'm betting he was the one who called her as soon as the body was found."

"Or he killed Dr. Hamstead, and she wants us to muddy the case," Jaxson tossed in.

I shivered at that thought, but the chill could be coming from the wind. "Let's hope that Sheila can help us find a clue."

I don't know why I was surprised that things were turning more complicated. They always did in a murder case. Just this once, though, why couldn't it be easy? After all, Jaxson, Rihanna, and I had fifty years advanced knowledge. That should count for something, right?

As soon as we stepped inside the library, a sense of calm surrounded me. While we had a library in Witch's Cove, this one was a lot nicer. Being in a college town probably helped.

I didn't see Mrs. Lawson anywhere, but I assumed she was

around. I know they used card catalogues back in the seventies, but I had no idea how to use one.

"What are we going to ask her?" Rihanna asked.

"I want to know if there are any newspaper or magazine articles about Richard Ashton. If he owned a local hotel, there should be photos of him at least. What good that will do, I don't know."

"Can I help you?" said a voice I recognized. I spun around and smiled. Her eyes widened. "Oh, it's you! Glinda, right?"

We had introduced ourselves last night. "Yes. And you remember Rihanna and Jaxson, of course."

I swear her cheeks turned pink. "Oh, my yes."

Really? Was there anyone immune to his charms? Right now, I couldn't worry about it. "We were wondering if you could point us in the direction of some information about Richard Ashton."

"Ashton? What do you need to know? I might be able to help."

I had no idea if Sheila would be unbiased, but I was willing to give her a try. No telling what stories Mrs. Tully had told her. "Things like what he invested in, what kind of man he was. Things like that."

"Let's sit at the table. Richard Ashton had a love of books. When his wife was alive, the two of them would come in here often."

"You knew him personally then?" I asked.

"More like on a professional level."

"What was he like?" Rihanna asked, acting rather enchanted.

Sheila smiled. "Wonderful, at least while his wife was

alive. He made his big money investing in ships, or rather barges, that traveled up and down the Ohio river. With that money, he invested in a few coal mines, and eventually bought the hotel downtown."

"He was generous?" I asked, though I don't know why it would matter. Sissy had claimed he was, but another opinion never hurt.

"Very, that is, until Susan died. Her death devastated him. We all reached out, but when any of us showed up at the house, his butler would answer and say that Mr. Ashton was indisposed."

A butler? My pulse shot up. "What was this butler's name?"

"Lou Kennedy, but he's passed away."

That was a shame. "Did he have any relatives that might be in town?"

"His grandson, Campbell Kennedy, lives here. In fact, he owns Charlotte's Pub on Third Street."

"I might stop in," I said.

"Do you believe in the myth that he stashed his wealth in the form of diamonds and gold?" Jaxson asked.

Sheila nodded. "If I believe Josephine, it's hidden somewhere in the mansion."

"Josephine?"

"Excuse me. Josephine Tully. I'm convinced the only reason she and her husband bought the old Ashton house was to find the treasure."

"Did she ever find any?" Rihanna asked, seemingly entranced with the fairy tale story.

Sheila chuckled. "Hardly. After Arnie died, I tried to

convince her to sell the old place, but she said she wouldn't until she found at least one diamond."

"A woman after my own heart," I said. "If you want something, you have to go after it."

"That sounds like Josephine all right."

A couple came into the library. Not wanting to keep Mrs. Lawson, I thanked her for her help. When she left, I looked over at Rihanna. "Would you like to add anything?"

"No."

"You believed she was being truthful."

"I guess. When a person is talking the whole time, they aren't having a lot of deep internal thoughts."

I smiled. "Fair enough."

"What do you say we head over to Charlotte's Pub?" Jaxson said.

"That's a great idea. I just hope it's open."

He looked down at his wrist, but he wasn't wearing a watch. "Anyone know what time it is?"

"No, and trust me, I miss my phone more than you can imagine," I said.

"What about me?" Rihanna kind of whined. "I'm a teenager."

We all chuckled. "If it's on Third Street, it should be easy to find. Or at least I hope it is."

Jaxson smiled. "If nothing else, it will be great exercise to help wear off all that food we packed in yesterday."

"Amen to that."

We headed out, and with the sun out, it wasn't as cold as before. Finding Charlotte's Pub was easy. Having a town laid out in a grid pattern was wonderful. And to our delight, the place was open.

As soon as we stepped inside, the smell of mildew almost knocked me over. The walls were made of faux stone and the floor of scarred wood. Oh, my.

Jaxson leaned over. "I think they were trying to make you think you are inside a coal mine."

I had to laugh. "All they need is a canary in a cage, though with the mold in here, I think he'd be dead in a week."

"Be nice." Jaxson nodded to the man behind the bar. "I wonder if that is Campbell Kennedy."

The three of us grabbed a booth. Menus sat in a clip on the table, which implied this was a bit more than just a bar.

The man behind the counter came over. He was nice looking with kind eyes and was about thirty-five years old.

"Welcome to Charlotte's Pub. Name's Campbell. What can I get you?"

Score! I felt a little funny coming out and just asking for information. Ordering some food would go a long way to greasing the wheel, so to speak. "I'd like a coffee and maybe some chips and salsa to share."

"You got it."

Rihanna and Jaxson also ordered coffee. When he left, I leaned toward them. "How do we bring up his grandfather without looking too nosy?"

"Since when does being nosy stop you?" Jaxson asked.

He was right. "If this had been Witch's Cove, I wouldn't have a problem."

Before I could come up with an approach, Campbell returned with our coffee and chips.

"Will you be ordering something off the menu?" he asked.

"I haven't decided."

"Take your time. What brings you to Charlotte?"

Since no one else was in the pub, he was probably bored. I went through the routine of Rihanna thinking about attending college here. "We're staying at the Ashton B&B."

"Oh, yeah? My grandfather used to work there."

That gave us the opening I was looking for. "Really? That place is so picturesque. Did he like it?" I thought my question was encouraging enough to make him want to talk.

"At first. Richard Ashton was a great employer until his wife died. Then it was like he became possessed."

I'd never met anyone who'd truly been possessed, but I'd seen enough television shows that depicted it. "What do you mean?"

"My grandfather worked for the man as his butler for thirty years, but when Mrs. Ashton died, Richard Ashton became angry, distant, and demanding. According to my grandfather, his boss made him do everything."

"Like what?"

"Shop, buy him clothes, take care of the bills. You name it. Ashton did have a woman who cleaned the house, so that helped."

"Why didn't your grandfather quit?"

"I asked him that question many times. He said it was because he felt sorry for Mr. Ashton. In reality, I think he was hoping he'd get a little inheritance when the old man died."

"He didn't?"

"Not a dime. I helped him out the best I could, but he died a broken man."

"That is terrible."

Campbell seemed to snap out of his tirade. "Sorry. I didn't mean to bring you down. Enjoy your coffee and just wave if you want to order anything."

"If I may ask you one more thing? You said that Richard Ashton had a maid. Is she still alive?"

"No. Her family tried to help her, also, but she was broken after what she called *the betrayal*, the same as my granddad."

"That is a shame."

He nodded and returned to the bar. The three of us sipped our coffee as I thought about whether his information would help us solve the case. Before I'd wrapped my mind around my thoughts, a group of people who looked to be college aged kids, piled in. Most likely, they were from town.

Between the chairs scraping against the hardwood floor and the sudden burst of music, I felt Campbell wouldn't hear us if we talked.

"Thoughts?" I asked.

"I feel sorry for his grandfather. If I'd worked for that many years and wasn't rewarded, I'd be a bit upset," Rihanna said.

"Me, too. I wonder if either the grandfather or the maid ever knew where he hid his money."

"Assuming he really had any, and if he hid it at all," Jaxson said.

"He didn't keep it in a bank, or so we were told."

"True." Jaxson asked.

"I say we order lunch and pick Campbell's brain again," I said. "He might know about Ashton's bank phobia."

After we chose our simple fare, Jaxson waved to get the owner's attention. Campbell trotted over. "Ready to order lunch?"

"Yes." I asked for a hamburger, which I thought they couldn't mess up too much, while Jaxson and Rihanna ordered one of the specials. "I can't remember who told us, but someone said that Mr. Ashton didn't believe in banks. Did your grandfather ever mention anything about that?"

"He mentioned that Ashton didn't trust banks. Where he put his wealth is anyone's guess."

"Maybe he hid stacks of money in his house," I suggested.

Campbell smiled. "Anything's possible."

So much for that line of questioning. "I have no idea why it matters, but what was the maid's name? The one who worked alongside of your grandfather."

"Cheryl Truscott, but as I said, she died two years ago."

"This is such a shame. Mr. Ashton didn't have any heirs then?"

"No. It was just him and his wife, which was what made him turn inward."

"Thanks, Campbell."

"You bet. I'll put the order in. Food will be right up." He spun around and headed back to the bar.

"Do you think knowing Ashton's history will help solve Dr. Hamstead's murder?" Jaxson asked.

"Maybe. Maybe not. I think it totally depends on why someone killed Hamstead."

"What do you think happened?" Jaxson asked.

I smiled. "If I knew that, I probably would be a psychic instead of a sleuth."

Jaxson cracked up. "Perhaps we should consult Madam Criant. I think she knows more than she's letting on."

"I totally agree."

Chapter Ten

THE PROBLEM WITH Jaxson's suggestion of visiting our resident psychic to find out who she suspected of Dr. Hamstead's murder, was that I didn't know if Madam Criant would willingly tell us much. She seemed secretive and probably for a good reason. I hadn't sensed anything evil radiating off her either time we'd met, but I've been wrong before.

One problem could be If Madam Criant didn't want my cousin to learn any of her secrets, she might be able to block her thoughts.

On the other hand, I was game for checking her out.

We headed out of the pub and walked one block toward the water. I should have asked Madam Criant how long she'd lived in Charlotte. If it was for any length of time, she must have heard the stories surrounding Richard Ashton and his later years, especially if she had been friends with Mrs. Tully and her cook for a while.

When we reached her storefront, the lights were out, but that didn't mean she wasn't there. I knocked and waited for her to emerge from the back. After a minute of standing in the freezing cold, I admitted defeat. I spun around to face Jaxson and Rihanna. "I guess we're on our own."

"Let's head back to the B&B and regroup then," he said.

"Works for me. I could use some warmth."

Now that we'd walked around the town a few times, I was getting a feel for where things were located. The numbered streets ran parallel to the river and the named streets were perpendicular. Someone had been thinking when they designed the town.

When we reached the B&B, a cruiser was parked in front. "What do you think that means?"

"Let's find out," Jaxson said.

The three of us headed inside. The deputy was in the smaller room with Mrs. Tully. Just then, the sheriff came downstairs with Stephanie Carlton in handcuffs. What?

I probably should keep my mouth shut, but I couldn't help myself. "You're arresting her?" Sure, that was an obvious conclusion, but I didn't know what else to ask. "Do you have proof of her guilt?"

"Ms. Goodall, is it?"

"Yes."

"Mrs. Carlton's fingerprints were found on the tea cup that held the poison that killed Dr. Hamstead."

My mind raced. Poison? That would mean he didn't die from blunt force trauma to the head. "Maybe someone framed her."

"You, perhaps?" he shot back.

"No." And he knew it too.

Jaxson draped an arm around my shoulders and guided me to the side. "Let's let the law take care of it, dear."

Fortunately, my common sense allowed me to keep my mouth shut for a change. If Stephanie had killed Hamstead, that meant we hadn't helped solve the case even the tiniest bit. How were we supposed to return back to the twenty-first century then?

Questions, questions. I had so many of them with few answers in sight.

The three of us went upstairs. As soon as we stepped into my room, I faced them. "How did they work so fast?" I asked.

"What do you mean?" Jaxson slipped off his jacket and slung it over the back of the sofa, while Rihanna and I tossed our outer gear on the bed.

"If they knew the drink had been poisoned, they must have tested it," I said.

"Wouldn't that mean they'd already performed the autopsy?" Rihanna asked. "They would have needed to make sure that specific poison was in Mr. Hamstead's system."

She was smart. "As I just said, they must have worked fast. I'm not buying it though."

"Why not?" Iggy asked as he crawled off his heating pad and waddled toward us. I reached down and picked him up. I figured he'd appreciate my body heat. The room wasn't the warmest.

"Something seems fishy about all of this." I snapped my fingers. "Maybe we're in a time warp and things are moving at a different speed from what we're used to."

"Huh?" Jaxson asked.

"All I'm saying is that we don't know how thorough autopsies were back in 1972. For all we know, the cup smelled of poison and the sheriff told the medical examiner just to check the victim's stomach contents."

"Possibly," he said. "Regardless, the sheriff thinks that

Stephanie is guilty. There must be a motive."

Rihanna stood. "I'm going to talk to Mrs. Tully. She and I have a bond."

I figured it couldn't do any harm. "Be careful."

Rihanna grinned and rushed out of the room.

"The sheriff has to be very good or really lucky if he can solve a crime in a day or two," Jaxson said.

"I agree. The question I'd like answered is why kill Dr. Hamstead? Those two had to have known each other, and yet she never mentioned that they did. You don't just poison a stranger."

"That's an excellent point. I'm hoping Mrs. Tully can shed some light on it."

"Perhaps his two students can too," I said. "I saw them in the sitting room. I'll see if they are surprised or relieved about who the suspected murderer is."

"Why would they be relieved? Is it because one of them could be the guilty party, and now, the spotlight is off him?" he asked.

"Yes, but remember, Stephanie Carlton is innocent until proven guilty. It is possible that she had tea with Dr. Hamstead and then someone came in to refresh his tea, and that tea was laced with poison."

Jaxson leaned back on the sofa. "You have one wild imagination."

"All one needs is reasonable doubt."

His brows pinched together. "Why are you so determined to prove this woman isn't guilty?"

I had to think about that for a moment. "Because we are meant to solve this case."

His brows rose. "Because some psychic told you we would—or rather we needed to?"

"Yes."

"That's putting a lot of faith in Madam Criant. Glinda, just because she pretended to believe that we were from the future doesn't mean she has the power to send us back. Even you said that."

"Yes, but now I want to change my mind. I'm allowed to, you know. The thought of staying here for the rest of my life is a bit depressing."

Jaxson scooted next to me and pulled me close. Iggy crawled over to Jaxson's lap, and I had to laugh.

"Think of the bright side," he said. "If we get stuck here, you could see snow every Christmas."

"Whoopee! And then what? Get a job waitressing at the River Bend Café? It's not like I can prove I went to college."

"Not unless the witch who sent us here altered your educational records."

Iggy lifted his head. "I would die if I had to stay here."

I petted his head. "I know, buddy. If you can think of a way for us to get back, let us know."

"Do you think I ruined things by eating the mistletoe?"

He sounded almost pathetic, and I didn't want him to feel guilty. "I hope not."

Rihanna charged in. "I learned a few things."

Finally, some good news. "Tell us."

She plopped down across from us. "Stephanie admitted that she was interested in Dr. Hamstead."

"To be husband number four?" I asked.

"I guess. She said she had tea with Dr. Hampstead the

night he died, but that when she left around ten o'clock, he was very much alive."

"Did Mrs. Tully say where Stephanie got the tea?" I asked. "Did she make it herself in the kitchen or what?"

"I didn't ask."

"Okay." I suppose I should jot down these questions in case we ran into the sheriff. "Anything else?"

"You will never ever guess who her mother is."

"Who Stephanie Carlton's mother is?" Where was she going with this?

"Yes."

"Rihanna," Jaxson said with a slight edge to his voice.

"Okay. This is exciting. Remember we learned that Richard Ashton had two servants, one a butler and the other a maid?"

"Yes, and both have passed."

"True, but the maid, Cheryl Truscott, was Stephanie's mother. According to Mrs. Tully, Ms. Carlton is very bitter toward Mr. Ashton because of the way he treated her mother at the end."

"That would be a good motive to kill Ashton, but what does that have to do with Dr. Hamstead?"

Rihanna held up a hand. "Just as I was about to ask her, I could hear a few words."

"What were they?" I asked.

"*Diamonds* and *found*."

"Diamonds? Could it be that Mrs. Tully is consumed with the idea of diamonds, and her thoughts had nothing to do with Ms. Carlton?"

"I guess," Rihanna said, as she dipped her chin.

"I have an idea," Jaxson said. "As long as we're throwing out crazy ideas that we don't have any proof of, what about the idea that Mrs. Tully overheard someone say that Dr. Hamstead found the stash of diamonds. Wanting to find out if there was any truth to it, Mrs. Tully sent in the much younger Ms. Carlton to seduce him."

"Now who is the one with the overactive imagination?" I asked.

"How else do you explain Rihanna's hearing those two words?"

He always did like to stump me. "I can't, but if Mrs. Tully has been searching this house for thirty years, I doubt someone who's merely a visitor could find them so quickly."

"Where are the diamonds now?" Iggy asked.

"Good question. If what Mrs. Tully suspects is true, they would have been on Dr. Hamstead's body, or else Stephanie stole them after she poisoned him—assuming she is guilty," I said. "I know, I know, I thought she was innocent, but I want to be open-minded."

Jaxson squeezed my shoulder. "If I'd found millions of dollars' worth of diamonds, I'd hide them until I had the chance to figure out what to do with them. And I certainly wouldn't just tell some random woman where they were located."

I reached across his body and stroked his cheek. "Not even if it was me?"

Yes, I was kidding, but it was always fun to see him squirm.

He smiled. "I guess for you I could make an exception."

"Aw, you are so sweet."

"Blah," Iggy said.

We all laughed. Footsteps sounded coming up the stairs. Before I could check it out, Rihanna jumped up. "Let me see who that is."

"It's probably the two men returning."

"Both of their rooms are before ours."

She had a point. Rihanna peaked out of the room. "You will not believe who it is."

"Stop with the guessing games." I admit I was a bit testy. "I'm sorry."

"No, I'm sorry. It was Stephanie Carlton."

I slipped out of Jaxson's grasp and stood. "The sheriff just arrested her. She should be in jail."

Rihanna shrugged. "What can I say? Unless they are letting her pack her things."

I'd never heard of anything like that, but I didn't know how things were done in the seventies. "Maybe Mrs. Tully said she wanted to rent the room and needed it cleared out."

"That kind of makes sense," Rihanna said.

I walked over to the window. "Someone from the sheriff's department just drove off."

Jaxson stood. "Perhaps he left a deputy here, figuring it might take her an hour or so to pack."

I shook my head. "Why not just ask Mrs. Tully to pack her things for her, or did they decide Stephanie is not guilty after all?"

"Mrs. Tully confirmed that Stephanie Carson is hurting for money," Rihanna said.

I faced my cousin. "Wasn't she the chatty one, though I believe Stephanie already mentioned that fact to Jaxson."

"My bad. I heard her think that. She didn't tell me directly, but this time I got the whole sentence, or at least most of it."

I had no idea what to make of it. "Maybe her daughter paid for her bail?"

"That makes more sense," Jaxson said.

"How about we all go down to the sitting room and see what other tidbits we can pick up?"

"You and Jaxson go ahead," Rihanna said. "I think I've had enough snooping for one day."

That wasn't like her, but I certainly didn't want to push. "Okay."

Jaxson and I slipped out of the room to go downstairs. "What are you hoping to learn?" he asked.

I was beginning to dislike that question. "I'd love to know why Stephanie was released, and secondly, is there any truth to Dr. Hamstead finding the diamonds?"

"Who do you think will tell you?" He held up a hand. "Anyone who admits to knowing the whereabouts of the diamonds is practically admitting he or she had something to do with the man's death. From all accounts, those diamonds could be worth millions—at least in our time."

Why did he always have to see through my logic? "Then how about enjoying a lovely afternoon sitting in front of the fire?"

He grinned. "You are so transparent, I should call you Ms. Cellophane."

I punched him and then headed to the sitting room.

Chapter Eleven

LUCK WAS ON our side, because the two PhD students were in the sitting room drinking coffee. I spotted the pot on the counter and poured myself and Jaxson some.

Since the men were in two of the four chairs surrounding the roaring fire—a spot where I wanted to be—we moved over there. "Mind if we join you?" I asked.

"Not at all," Dominic said.

We sat to their right, and I immediately sipped my coffee and groaned. "This hits the spot."

Jaxson tasted his. "It is good."

I set my cup on my lap and twisted toward the men. "Did you guys see that Stephanie Carlton has returned? I thought the sheriff arrested her for murder." Not wanting anyone who might be lurking in the hall to overhear, I kept my voice low.

Both men nodded. "Maybe the sheriff realized he didn't have enough evidence to hold her," Phil said.

"Why not keep her overnight at least?" That was what Steve Rocker would have done. Then again, I was not up on my 1970's police protocols.

"The evidence that came to light must have been pretty persuasive," Dominic said.

I leaned forward. "Like what? I doubt someone walked

into the station and confessed."

Dominic chuckled. "No, I imagine not, but I heard the sheriff's department found a bottle of rum in Michael's room. I bet when they tested the contents, it changed their minds."

"Are you saying the rum could have been poisoned?"

Phil shrugged. "Suppose it was? It's possible that after Stephanie left Michael's room, he poured some of the liquor into his teacup and drank from it. Michael loved his rum."

"Then the cup would have traces of it. Surely, they would have known that before they arrested her, right?"

"I couldn't say. There are only two people who might know the answer. One would be the sheriff and the other Stephanie, assuming they told her anything."

"How do you know she didn't just make bail?" Jaxson asked.

"For a murder case? No way."

I always thought that if a person wasn't a flight risk, they could remain in their home. "Maybe she's wearing an ankle monitor that lets the sheriff know if she tries to leave here."

The two men looked at each other and then back at me. "What's an ankle monitor?"

Oh, no. I just let something slip about an item made in the future.

"What Glinda is trying to say, is that maybe they will have someone monitor her to make sure she doesn't leave the house." Jaxson to the rescue again.

"Yes, that's what I meant. My mind is whirling. I'm still a bit upset over being in a house where someone died."

I had to remember not to mention my parents ran a funeral home—one that was situated below where I grew up. I could only hope the sheriff didn't mention it to these guys.

"I can understand that. Every time I look across the hallway, I expect to see Michael come out of his room." Dominic turned his attention to the fire and stared. At first glance, it looked like he really was upset.

"I heard mention of some diamonds." I was hoping to stimulate the conversation.

Phil chuckled. "That old tale? If Richard Ashton hid diamonds in the house, they would have been found already."

"Who's to say there isn't some super-secret compartment where he hid them?" I asked. "Maybe Dr. Hamstead got lucky and found it."

Phil shook his head. "I've heard Mrs. Tully all but pulled up the floorboards looking for them."

"You're right." I then studied the fire, enjoying its heat. "Did either of you hear what the sheriff thought Stephanie's motive was for killing Dr. Hamstead? That's assuming she really did kill him."

"No, but Michael told me that the two of them were really hitting it off," Dominic said.

If Stephanie sincerely liked him, that was a shame. "That's tough."

"If Stephanie didn't kill him, do either of you have a suspect?" Jaxson asked.

They looked at each other and shrugged. "No. We were only supposed to be here for a semester, so it wasn't as if Michael was a threat to any teacher here," Dominic said.

I hadn't thought about someone working at the college wanting him dead. "Could someone have snuck into the house after hours?" I asked. "Mrs. Tully assured us the front door would be locked at ten each night."

"Maybe there is another entrance," Dominic said.

My mind raced. "There is a door to the outside through the kitchen. Maybe the cook forgot to lock it."'

"It's possible, but as I said, no teacher's job was threatened. Michael was here on exchange."

"That does seem unlikely that another professor would want him gone. How long have you three been here?" I asked.

"About ten days. We wanted to get a feel of the town and find a place to rent. Christmas is not the best time for real estate agents to be available, which is why we are staying here until we find something," Phil said.

That all sounded logical. "I hope the sheriff finds out who killed your friend and why."

"Me, too."

I wished Rihanna had come with us so she could read their minds.

"Let's head upstairs," Jaxson said. "I don't want to keep Rihanna waiting."

I wondered why he thought she would be, but I didn't want to question him in front of these men. I stood. "Gentlemen."

Jaxson and I traipsed upstairs. I was very curious as to why he wanted to stop short the conversation. When we entered my room, I found Rihanna on the bed reading a book.

She closed the book and sat up. "Did you learn anything?"

I gave her the rundown. "I still kinda get of a weird vibe off these guys, but I don't think they are murderers." I turned to Jaxson. "What's your take?"

"They said nothing that would raise a red flag for me."

I plopped down on the sofa. "I'd really like to pick Stephanie's brain."

"Glinda."

I knew that tone. "I won't confront her until after we know she's no longer a suspect."

"Good, though I'm convinced someone in this house killed Dr. Hamstead," he said.

"How about we check to see when the registrar will be in the office?" Rihanna asked. "They might be able to give us some idea what Dr. Hamstead was like. Someone had to have interviewed him."

My cousin never ceased to amaze me. "It's possible they are open today. How about we check it out and then grab dinner?"

"You just want to pick Sissy's brain at the River Bend Café," Jaxson said with a chuckle.

"There's nothing wrong with that. Different sources provide different insights."

He grinned. "That's my girl. Grab your jackets, ladies."

While I'd love to include Iggy, he would not fare well outside. "Would you like us to let you roam?" I asked.

"How long will you be gone?"

"It could be a couple of hours." He couldn't stay cloaked for that long and remaining hidden wasn't his thing either.

"That's okay. Just bring me back some food."

"Can do."

The three of us headed out. On the walk over, we practiced what Rihanna was going to say. Luckily, the college wasn't far from the Ashton B&B, so I wasn't frozen to the bone when I arrived. Finding the admissions office was a bit of a challenge until we located a student who gave us directions.

To our delight, someone was manning the office. No secretary was out front, so we knocked on her door. The older woman looked up, smiled, and then motioned us in.

"We're sorry to barge in like this without an appointment, but we only have a few days in Charlotte, and my cousin here is interested in Charlotte College for the fall."

"Great. Pull up a chair. It's dead around here, so I'm happy for the distraction."

The name plate read Sonia Tisdale. "Thanks."

"How can I help you?"

Rihanna went through her spiel about loving photography, but she also thought that business made more sense. "I heard that a Dr. Hamstead was going to be a guest teacher this year. One of my friends from Embry-Tucker had him and said he was great."

"Dr. Hamstead?"

The confused look on her face had my pulse elevating. "He and his two PhD students are supposed to be teaching here. Something about the feasibility of products moving up and down the Ohio River."

I really should have questioned Dominic and Phil more about what Dr. Hamstead would be teaching.

Sonia Tisdale flipped through a book and then shook her head. "I'm sorry. I don't have any listing for him. Was he to teach in the business department?"

"History," Rihanna said.

She checked again with the same result. Since we'd

learned what we'd come for, there was no use in staying, but we didn't want to appear rude.

"We probably were mistaken," I said.

Rihanna asked a few more questions and then picked up a brochure. "Thank you for your time. You have a beautiful campus."

"We think so too, but if you ever get the chance to visit here in the spring or fall, you will love it. It's lush and peaceful."

Once we left, we regrouped outside. "What do you think?" I asked.

"If anyone would know about Dr. Hamstead, it would be the registrar," Jaxson said.

"Maybe it was a last-minute hire," I said trying to think of some reason for his name not being on the register.

His brows rose. "Let's see what Sissy has to say. We can always return tomorrow and speak to someone in the history department."

"It's possible they weren't here to teach," I said.

"If not to teach, then what?" Jaxson asked.

"I have no basis for my theory, but maybe Dr. Hamstead was here to look for the diamonds," I suggested.

Jaxson laughed. "You believe that? No treasure has been found in thirty years, and you think Dr. Hamstead expected to show up for a week or two and find it?"

"Anything's possible. He's a history professor. Maybe people have written about it, or he could have located the original house plans and found there is a secret compartment somewhere."

The slight tilt of Jaxson's head implied I'd hit a nerve.

"Why didn't Mrs. Tully or her husband think of that?"

"I guess we could ask her, but she might be too embarrassed to tell the truth."

"Guys, it's cold standing here. How about we head to town?" Rihanna said.

What had I been thinking? My mind often blocked my physical discomfort when I had a brainstorm.

"Let's go," Jaxson said.

For the next few minutes, we traveled in silence. That worked for me since I needed time to think. By the time we arrived at the café, I was more convinced that I was on to something.

We stepped inside, and the relief from the cold was very welcome. Adding to my excitement was that Sissy was working. She looked up and smiled.

"Take a seat. I'll be right over," she called from across the room.

This time, her café was at least half full. We piled into a booth, but I didn't remove my jacket just yet. I wasn't sure I'd ever be warm again.

A minute later, Sissy came over with her pad in hand. "Nice to see you again." Her smile turned into a frown. "I heard there was a tragedy at the B&B."

I was thrilled she was on top of things. "Yes. Terrible thing. Poor Dr. Hamstead was poisoned."

"Any idea why someone would want him dead?" she asked.

I couldn't tell if she knew something and didn't want to spill the beans, or if she wanted the gossip. It wasn't as if I knew much. "The sheriff arrested one of the guests, but released her shortly thereafter."

"I heard more evidence came to light."

I sat up straighter. Who had told her? Was there a gossip in the sheriff's department like there was in Witch's Cove? "Do you know what that was?"

"Something about the accused claimed she heard the victim arguing with someone a little while after she left Dr. Hamstead's room."

"She could have made that up," Jaxson said.

"True."

As much as this line of questioning might be helpful, I wasn't sure Sissy could provide answers. "I have a question for you. If someone wanted to get their hands on the architectural plans for a house, where would they go?"

"Mary Reynolds is a secretary over at the courthouse. Everyone who has a home on the Preservation Society roster has to register their blueprints. Why?"

I liked Sissy and saw no reason not to tell her my hare-brained idea. "Who's to say someone didn't get a hold of the plans and learn of a secret hiding place—a place where diamonds might have been stored? Maybe Dr. Hamstead found them, and the killer caught him in the act."

Sissy sucked in a breath. "Oh, my. That belongs in a mystery novel."

I laughed. "That would be a good one."

"Talk to Mary. She'll know where to direct you if she doesn't have the plans."

"You've been very helpful."

Sissy smiled. "I bet I can be more helpful by taking your order."

I grinned. She reminded me of Dolly Andrews in so many ways. "Let's start with three hot coffees."

"You got it."

My toes were tingling, a sure sign we were on the right track. Tomorrow would be an interesting day since we'd be stopping at the courthouse.

Chapter Twelve

THE NEXT MORNING, I was surprised and delighted to find Stephanie Carlton at breakfast. Sure, she had to eat, but I bet she could have asked to have her breakfast delivered to her room. If I'd been arrested for a crime, I probably would have hidden upstairs. On the other hand, if I was innocent, I might not.

While she probably would have preferred to be by herself, I wanted her to tell us to leave her alone. The three of us walked over. "Hey, Stephanie. Do you want some company?"

Her eyes were a bit red. She smiled, and her relief seemed sincere. "Yes, please. Maybe you can help this nightmare go away."

We all sat down. "Tell us what happened."

"I admitted that I kind of set my sights on Dr. Hamstead. After all, he was good looking, single, nice, and he had a good job."

"Money is tight, is it?" I asked, even though I knew the answer.

"You have no idea. When Burt died, he left me with very little. My second husband had a prolonged hospital stay that ate up our savings. When my mother became ill, I used up what savings we had."

Since she didn't mention this mother was Richard Ashton's maid, I let it be. "That had to be tough."

"It was."

"If I could be so nosy, why did the sheriff think you murdered Dr. Hamstead?"

"Like he said. He found my fingerprints on the tea cup. There was some poison in Michael's cup, so he figured I'd put it there."

"I can't imagine that would hold up in court. It's purely circumstantial," I threw out.

"I know. At the station, I told him that I'd heard someone talking to Michael in his room about an hour after I left. My room is next to his."

"Was it a man or a woman?" Jaxson asked.

"I couldn't tell." She huffed out a laugh. "I thought about knocking on the door and pretending I'd left something in his room, but I didn't want to look like the typical jealous woman."

"That would imply you didn't poison him, but why did the sheriff believe you? I mean, you could have been making it up."

"The lab tested the rum bottle in his room and found it contained the same poison."

"If Dr. Hamstead just died," Rihanna said, "How were they able to determine that so fast?" Was there some kind of litmus paper test for poison?

"Turns out the sheriff's wife is the medical examiner."

Are you kidding me? Can we say *conflict of interest*? "Handy. Does the sheriff have any idea who might have harmed the victim?"

"He was very tight-lipped."

Mrs. Tully carried over our breakfast. "Here you go."

"Thanks."

While I wanted to ask about the diamonds, I thought it best to eat first and think about how I wanted to bring up the topic afterward.

Rihanna spoke up. "In what department was Dr. Hamstead going to teach?"

"History."

I was surprised my cousin asked since she knew the answer.

"That's a shame. It would have been fun to take a class from someone I'd sort of met."

Stephanie nodded and then sipped her tea.

When I was halfway through my meal, I couldn't help but dig a little deeper. "Was Dr. Hamstead ever curious about the lore surrounding this place?"

"The lore?"

"The fact that Richard Ashton might have buried diamonds in the house."

Stephanie tilted her head. "We talked about it, just as I'm sure everyone who has ever stayed here has, but he wasn't about to go in the backyard in the dead of night and start digging up the lawn."

I had to chuckle at that image. The ground would be too hard for that. "Got it."

Either Stephanie really didn't know anything else, or else she was hiding something. Once we finished, we excused ourselves and returned to my room.

By now the courthouse would be open, and I was curious

to see what Mary in Records had to say about whether anyone had asked to view the plans of the old B&B. I also wondered if anyone could look at them. That is, were they open to the public? They might be if this house was on the Preservation list.

There was only one way to find out: ask her.

After layering on a few more shirts, and then tossing on our coats, which was getting to be a real pain, we went out. We had seen the courthouse on our many trips downtown. It was on Waverly Avenue between Second and Third Streets.

Inside, we followed the signs to the Records department. Because the population of Charlotte was only ten thousand, not many people were there. Thankfully, we only had to wait five minutes for Mary to be free.

"How can I help you?"

Since Mary seemed to be more interested in Jaxson, it made sense for him to ask the questions about the Ashton House.

After some flirting, and maybe a bit of begging, Mary admitted that she'd let a man by the name of Michael Hamstead look at the plans. The question was whether he'd found anything or not.

Because they were public record, she let us see them, too. I studied the downstairs plans, while Rihanna and Jaxson took the upstairs. Rihanna had already shown an affinity for being very visual, which meant she could look at something and retain the image. Being a math person, it was one of my talents as well.

Less than ten minutes into our search, Jaxson stepped back. "Thank you so much."

"Did you find what you were looking for?" Mary asked.

"I did."

He did? It was smart of him not to tell us in front of her. Who knows who she'd tell? I did love that Charlotte was quite similar to Witch's Cove.

Once outside, I had to ask. "What did you see?"

He grinned. "In the room where Michael Hamstead was staying, there is a false back to the bookcase."

"Do you think that Mr. Ashton hid his diamonds in there?"

"It's as good a guess as any. I'd bet anything that Dr. Hamstead searched for them. Whether he found them or not I couldn't say."

"How did Mrs. Tully not know about it?" I asked.

"Why would she? There were probably books on the shelves blocking her view. It's possible the house came furnished when she and her husband bought it."

"She still should have asked to look at the house plans," I said.

"I would have."

"It's a moot point now. Apparently, she didn't think of it. Let's suppose that Dr. Hamstead found the diamonds. He might have returned them to the hiding place until he could figure out where to put them."

A gust of wind snaked up my jacket. Okay, I couldn't live in a place that was this cold in the winter.

"Anything's possible," Jaxson said. "I'm hoping I can sneak into his room and check it out."

"What will you do if you find the diamonds?" Rihanna asked.

"They belong to Mrs. Tully. It's her house. I'll hand them over."

"Wouldn't you be tempted to take one?" she asked.

"Rihanna Samuels," I chastised. "That would be wrong."

My cousin shrugged. "It's not like anyone would know. When we get back to Witch's Cove, you could pawn it."

Jaxson chuckled. "I couldn't live with myself."

"Fine."

"Rihanna," I said. "Our goal here is to solve the case in order to get back to our time. Not profit from it."

"I know."

Once we returned to the B&B, we headed upstairs. The door to Dr. Hamstead's room was closed, but I didn't see any police tape across it. I doubted Mrs. Tully had rented the room yet, but as we passed, I twisted the knob. It failed to open. Darn.

As soon as we stepped into our room, Iggy roused. "Did you learn anything?" I gave him the rundown. "What are you waiting for?" he asked. "Let's check it out."

"I'd pick the lock, buddy, but I don't have my kit with me," Jaxson said.

"Then sneak the key out of Mrs. Tully's office. The keys are hanging on hooks above her desk in that office," Iggy said.

"Mrs. Tully is usually in there. I really don't want to have to explain if I get caught."

Iggy puffed out his chest. "Then I'll do it."

"You?" I asked.

"Don't look so surprised. Carry me downstairs in your purse. I'll cloak myself and crawl into her office. As soon as I touch the key it will disappear."

"It's heavy," I said not thinking he could do this.

"Try me," my cute little iguana challenged. "I'm strong."

I placed my room key on the floor. Picking it up from that position would be more difficult than taking it off a hook—or so I believed. Iggy failed the first two times, but he succeeded on the third attempt.

"See? I can do it."

I figured worst case scenario, he'd lift the key off the hook, and it would drop to the floor. If Mrs. Tully happened to be around, she might think Dr. Hamstead's ghost was trying to take it or something. There was no way she'd suspect I had a magical iguana who could become invisible.

"Let's do this."

Iggy knew the drill. He rushed over to my purse and jumped in. As casual as I could, I headed out the door. "Rihanna, would you mind joining me? We might need to create a distraction."

"Sure. This should be fun."

We walked into the sitting room since it was across the hall from Mrs. Tully's office and sat in the chairs close to the fireplace. I set my purse on the floor and let Iggy do his thing. I wanted to watch, but that might cause someone to ask what I was doing.

"I wish we had a fireplace in the office," I said in a voice loud enough to drown out what Iggy was about to do.

"I know, but Jaxson has one at his place, right?"

"Yes. There is nothing nicer than a roaring fire when you're cold."

I was glad no one was in the sitting room or else they'd wonder about our boring conversation. About four minutes later, my bag puffed up. Iggy was back.

"Did you get it?" I whispered.

"Of course, but it will cost you."

"The best I can do is lettuce." I hoped the cook wasn't in the kitchen so I could sneak in and grab some.

"Works for me."

Before we returned upstairs, I went into the kitchen, which thankfully was empty. I opened the fridge, found some lettuce, and grabbed a leaf. Considering they only made breakfast, I wasn't sure why they would even stock any, unless Mrs. Tully made lunch and dinner here, but I couldn't worry about that now.

Rihanna and I rushed out. I couldn't believe how hard my heart was beating. When we went into the room, I plastered my back against the door.

Jaxson jumped up. "Did something happen?"

"No, but stealing makes me nervous." I opened my purse and lifted Iggy out who was clutching the key. "You are amazing."

He wiggled his little body. "I know."

I placed him on the heating pad and gave him his reward. I then handed the key to Jaxson. "You'll have to do it. I don't know where this hiding place is."

That, and I was too nervous to go inside the dead man's room. I feared someone would catch me snooping and think I'd stolen and then hidden the diamonds.

"Coward." He grinned.

"Guilty as charged, but I'll stand outside the room and tap on the door if anyone is coming. Maybe you can hide."

He laughed. "You've seen too many movies. I'll be fine."

"What if someone catches you?" Knowing Jaxson, he wasn't thinking along those negative lines.

"Stop worrying."

Together we went to Dr. Hamstead's room, which hopefully hadn't been rented. Jaxson knocked. When no one answered, he let himself in. As soon as he stepped inside, I stood watch.

And waited.

Chapter Thirteen

I HAD NO idea how long Jaxson had been in Dr. Hamstead's room, but it seemed like an eternity. Eventually though, the door opened, and he emerged. With a quick nod, Jaxson turned and headed back to where our rooms were located. I trotted after him.

Why wasn't he saying anything? Sheesh. I swear he wanted to torture me. Once inside, he stood by the door, apparently waiting for everyone to listen.

"I found the hidden alcove, but there were no diamonds," he announced.

Darn. "Could you tell if anything had been in the hiding place?" I asked.

"How?"

"I imagine dust would have accumulated around the sack of diamonds. Did it look like anything had been moved?"

Jaxson pressed his lips together. "Not my thing, so no I didn't notice."

"I can go back," Iggy offered.

"That's okay. Diamonds might not have been what this murder was about anyway." I wish they had been. It would make the motive easier to understand.

Iggy puffed out his chest. "When I first saw the body in

there, I noticed gouge marks on the floor."

"The building is old, buddy," Jaxson said. "I bet if you look, you'll find gouge marks in here, too."

Rihanna eased off the bed. "Iggy might be onto something. What if before our history professor found out about the hidden compartment, he tore up the floorboards looking for the gems. Frustrated at not succeeding, he went to the courthouse to learn about a possible hidden space?"

"Assuming he found the diamonds, where would they be now? He certainly didn't expect to be murdered," Jaxson said.

"They could be anywhere," Rihanna said. "For all we know, the person who murdered him has them, or else he was in cahoots with his two apprentices and told them to hold onto the diamonds until they figured out how to fence them without getting caught."

My cousin was naïve. "Two young guys? They'd divide the diamonds in a heartbeat and leave town."

"I guess."

"I wouldn't," Jaxson said. "I'd hang low for a while to remove suspicion."

Since he'd been in jail for three years on a trumped-up charge, Jaxson might know about the criminal mind. "That would be smart, so now what?" I asked to no one in particular.

"Let me look around," Iggy begged again.

Jaxson said nothing, which implied we had nothing to lose. "Okay, but don't dawdle. We have to get the key back to Mrs. Tully's office."

Iggy did his little dance. "Thank you."

Jaxson lifted him up. "I'll take him in there."

I must have appeared nervous. "Thanks."

The two of them left. I assumed Iggy would cloak himself once in the hallway. We didn't need Jaxson having to explain why he had an iguana and then have Mrs. Tully say animals were prohibited. If we were forced to leave the B&B, we'd never stand a chance of solving this case.

Rihanna and I both picked up a book to read while we waited for them to return.

After ten minutes, Rihanna slammed shut her book. "What's taking them so long?"

"Iggy must be doing some kind of grid search. I should have asked Jaxson if Dr. Hamstead's clothes and belongings were still in there, though I can't imagine the sheriff's department leaving them. They'd want to look for clues—or for the stash of diamonds."

A forever time later, Jaxson returned with Iggy in his arms. "Iggy is the king!" he announced with pride.

I didn't expect that. "Do tell."

"Close your eyes and hold out your hand," Jaxson instructed.

I did as he asked. A moment later, something dropped into my palm. I opened my eyes and gasped. "A diamond? Where did you find this?"

"Under the desk," my familiar said.

"How do you think it got there?" I lifted up the gem and studied it. Not that I was any kind of expert, but to me, the brilliance of the stone was outstanding.

"The desk sits in front of the bookcase where the hidden cubbyhole is located," Jaxson said.

"Do you think someone dropped this by mistake?" That seemed like the most likely scenario.

"That would be my bet," Jaxson said.

"What do we do now?" I could think of a few options.

"The diamond probably belongs to Mrs. Tully, but I think we should take it to the sheriff. That might help focus his search on a thief," Jaxson said. "Or rather a murderous thief, assuming the same person who now has the diamonds killed Dr. Hamstead."

It was the right thing to do. "What did you do with the key?"

"We returned it. We don't need someone accusing us of stealing, or worse, murder. If I could sneak into Dr. Hamstead's room one time, someone might think I could have done it before."

"That's logical. I was about to say we should look up where the sheriff's department is located, but we don't have a computer. I never realized how much I'd come to rely on technology."

"You and me both," Rihanna said.

"Before we go, we should decide what we are going to tell the sheriff about how and where we found the diamond," I said.

Jaxson looked over at Iggy and then back at me. "Mostly the truth?"

"What would that be? That Iggy somehow snuck into the room, found the diamond, and understood it's value?"

He stabbed a hand over his head. "I guess not. It will be hard enough to admit Iggy is with us."

"You could say that you didn't want me to stay home alone. I can be a handful, you know, so you had to take me with you to Ohio." If Iggy could grin, he would be doing so right now.

I had a talented familiar. "That works, but how did you know to bring the diamond to us?"

No one said anything for a moment.

"I got it. Say it got stuck in between my toes." Iggy lifted his leg and wiggled his appendages.

"That's good. You got loose, wandered into the dead man's room, and stepped on the diamond. The question is when? The day Dr. Hamstead died or just now?"

"I couldn't go long with it in my toes," he said.

"Today then. We'll say the door wasn't locked," Jaxson said.

I shook my head. "But it's locked now."

"Do you think someone cleaned the room this morning?" Rihanna asked.

I looked over at Jaxson to see what he thought.

"It looked clean. In fact, it smelled like some lemon-scented cleaner."

I smiled. "That's perfect. When the maid, or Mrs. Tully, was cleaning, the door was open and our troublemaker wandered in, stepped on the diamond, and came out. We went out today and didn't notice it until just now."

Jaxson's gaze shifted to the side. "I like that. Should we take Iggy with us to prove we have an iguana?"

"I'll leave that up to Iggy. Are you ready to brave the cold if I wrap you up really good?"

"I can't talk to the sheriff, but I'm game if you just need to prove I exist."

"We do. It's not like I can take a selfie with the two of us and show him." I really missed my cell phone. Life without technology was proving to be a challenge.

I wrapped him up until he could barely move and then placed him in my purse. We would head downtown and ask someone where to find the sheriff's department. Hopefully, his office wasn't too far from the center of town.

The walk was rather nice since the air was a bit warmer today. Turns out our destination was on Second Street, rather close to Madam Criant's shop.

Our luck held when we were able to get in to see the sheriff without much explanation. Once in Sheriff Filmore's office, he pushed back his chair and stood. "Glinda, is it?"

"Yes." We introduced ourselves again, and then sat in the chairs in front of his desk.

"What brings you here?"

"We found this at the Ashton B&B." I placed the diamond on his desk.

No surprise, his eyes widened. "Where did you get this exactly?"

I told him how Iggy got loose and wandered into Dr. Hamstead's room. "It was stuck in between his toes. He hobbled back, and I removed it."

"You have an iguana?"

Expecting his disbelief, I eased Iggy out of my purse. "I do. I didn't want to leave him alone in Florida. He has a tendency to get into trouble."

"Oh, my. Does he bite?"

"He never has." Though I wouldn't put it past him if someone irritated him.

"Let me get this straight. Your pet found the diamond?"

I'd just said that.

"Yes," Jaxson answered. "That prompted us to wonder if this was but one of the many hidden—in theory—diamonds once owned by Richard Ashton."

"Is that so?" the sheriff asked deadpan.

"Yes. We thought there might be some kind of secret compartment in the room. Otherwise, Mrs. Tully would have found the stash years ago."

I couldn't help myself from speaking up. "That's when we thought to check the county records' department." I explained about us asking to see the floorplan of the house and then how we learned that Dr. Hamstead had also enquired about it.

"Did you find this hidden storage spot?" the sheriff asked.

"Yes. At least on paper we did. It's in the bookcase behind the desk," I said. "I'm thinking Dr. Hamstead could have found the diamonds and then was killed because he refused to tell the killer where they were."

"Fascinating. I'll be sure to have someone check there for the diamonds."

He didn't ask where this hiding place was exactly, so he must be planning to ask Mary about it. I didn't tell him not to bother, that we had already looked and had come up empty-handed, because it would raise too many unwanted questions. The idea that we'd done some breaking and entering might not go over well with him.

"If you find the diamonds, will you return them to Mrs. Tully?" I asked.

"When the case is resolved, I'll make sure they get back to their rightful owner."

When Sheriff Filmore nodded, I figured that was his way of saying we were excused. I honestly didn't know what I thought he'd do about our find, but we had done our civic duty. The ball was in his court now, so to speak.

Once we left, none of us said much. That worked for me since I didn't want to dawdle. I was sure Iggy was cold, despite being wrapped up. When we reached the B&B, I was a little unsettled mostly because this case seemed to be going nowhere. More than ever, I was convinced we might never leave Charlotte, Ohio, especially if our return to Witch's Cove depended on figuring out who killed Dr. Hamstead.

We were half way up the stairs when a hallway door opened. I swear it sounded like it was coming from the room that had been rented to the dead man, but we couldn't see from where we were standing. Was a maid in there cleaning again, or had someone overheard us talking about the diamond and wanted to see if there were more?

While I wanted to wait on the stairwell to see who came out, that would be bad if we were caught. When we reached the landing, I looked around, but all of the doors were closed. Darn.

As soon as we stepped into our room, I lifted Iggy from my purse and placed him on the heating pad, leaving the towel he'd been wrapped in next to him in case he wanted to use it. "Did anyone else hear someone go into Dr. Hamstead's room?" I asked.

"I heard something," Iggy said as he flattened his body on the pad in order to get the maximum heat.

"Glinda, I know you," Jaxson said. "Please don't go knocking on the door. How about I go back to my room and leave the door cracked a bit? I'll watch to see who comes out," Jaxson said.

His room was closer to Hamstead's room than mine. "Great."

"Take me!" Iggy said.

"Why?" I asked.

"When the person who is in the room leaves, I can peak my head out. No one is going to believe that I talk and can squeal on them."

I chuckled. "That might work." I turned back to Jaxson. "How about taking his heating pad with you."

"Can do. I imagine it will take a while if there is a person inside. He or she might be cleaning or looking for the rest of the diamonds."

"The more I think about it, the more convinced I am that the killer already took them," Rihanna said.

"Is there something you aren't telling us?" I asked. She could read minds. "We all thought that Hamstead would have hidden them. It's not like he's going to invite someone in for tea and set them out on the table for the killer to find."

"If that were true, how do you explain the cubbyhole being empty—besides thinking Dr. Hamstead gave them to his two apprentices?" she shot back.

Jaxson stepped up. "The tea drinker, aka Stephanie Carlton, could have been in on it with him."

That was another intriguing twist. "You might be right. I always did find it odd that she could get so cozy with Dr. Hamstead in such a short period of time."

Rihanna shrugged. "She's attractive enough to be successful. All she had to do was suggest she was willing to do him a few favors and boom—an evening invite to tea."

"Rihanna Samuels!"

"What? They're in the nineteen-seventies, and from what I've read, since the sixties, it was all about love and peace."

"And war, but that's not important."

"We'll let you know what we find." Jaxson smiled, grabbed Iggy and his heating pad, and left for their surveillance duty.

Rihanna stood and headed toward the door. "I'm going downstairs to look for something to read. The books here are boring. I noticed there were some pretty coffee table photo books in the sitting room."

I'd seen them, too. "Want company?"

She smiled. "I'm good. Come get me if and when Jaxson reports back."

"Okay." I thought it a bit odd that she suddenly wanted to check them out, but I know photography brought her some comfort.

Rihanna stepped into the hallway. Just as I was closing the door, another door across the hall opened. I wanted to look, but that might be a bit suspicious. Rihanna could handle whatever came her way, but if she needed help, Jaxson would be by her side in a flash.

Being totally nosy, I pressed my ear to the door, but I couldn't make out the words. All I could tell was that Rihanna was speaking conversationally.

Frustrated, I plopped down on the bed, waiting for Jaxson and Iggy to report back.

Chapter Fourteen

A MINUTE LATER, Jaxson knocked, and then he and Iggy entered my room.

I jumped off the bed. "Who was in Dr. Hamstead's room?"

"Dominic."

Not who I would have guessed. "So much for being a friend in mourning."

"I saw Rihanna talking to him."

Iggy, who was sitting on Jaxson's shoulder, lifted his head. "Do you want me to follow this guy?"

I shook my head. "No. I don't think he's going anywhere." I'm not sure why I said that. I couldn't be sure what his plans were.

"Where was Rihanna off to?" Jaxson asked.

"To look at some photo books. We didn't know when you were going to be back."

"I'll go downstairs and let her know Dr. Hamstead's room is no longer occupied." He handed Iggy off to me, along with the heating pad.

"Thanks."

I plugged in the pad and set Iggy on top. "I might have to get one of these for you at home—if we ever get there."

"I'd like that."

Jaxson returned a few minutes later. "Rihanna was chatting with Mrs. Tully, so I didn't want to disturb her."

"She's a good detective. People like Mrs. Tully are often invisible to the guests. I'm hoping our owner has learned something about Dr. Hamstead's death during her wanderings."

He nodded. "I noticed she is often in the main sitting room refreshing the coffee and putting out cookies, and no one seems to pay attention to her."

Iggy lifted his head. "I heard something."

My familiar had great hearing. "What was it?"

"It came from downstairs."

"You can hear that far away?" I was suspect, but I stepped to the door and opened it up.

Jaxson moved next to me, and we both listened. "That's Rihanna's voice," he said.

"Can you make out what she is saying?"

"No."

"At least she is okay." I turned around, and when I stepped back into the room, my gaze shot straight to the heating pad. "Where's Iggy?"

Jaxson helped me look, but we came up empty. "I bet the little bugger slipped out."

"He had to have cloaked himself then or we would have seen him."

"Let's wait on the sofa for him and keep the door cracked so he can get back in. When Rihanna returns, we can plot our next move."

"I'm not good at waiting."

Jaxson chuckled. "Tell me something I don't know."

Because we wanted to stay put for when our two master sleuths returned, we snuggled on the sofa. I should be content just sitting there, being safe and warm with someone who was growing more and more dear to me, but when a case was looming, my mind refused to shut off.

When Rihanna eventually returned, she was holding up her hands. For a moment, I thought she might have cut her finger. I jumped up. "Are you hurt?"

"No, but I would be dead if I hadn't read Mrs. Tully's mind. Ugh. I am so mad that I misjudged her."

"Whoa. Slow down. Dry your hands and then tell us what happened."

"I can't dry them."

"Can't? Why not?"

She sat across from us, her hands not touching anything. "I was headed downstairs to look at the photo books, but before I made it to the stairs, Dominic came out of Dr. Hamstead's room. He was good at blocking his thoughts, but I sensed a hint of fear, like I'd caught him doing something."

"Like searching for the rest of the diamonds?" I asked.

"I thought it wise not to ask him. He could have been the one who killed Dr. Hamstead."

"He is definitely high on my suspect list," I said.

"Not mine. At least not anymore," she said.

She was driving me crazy. "Why not?"

The door eased open and then Iggy appeared. "Whew. I'm getting too old to climb up the banister while cloaked."

I huffed out a laugh. "I'm glad you recognize that."

Yes, I was kidding, but it was always fun to get in a jab.

Iggy was doing it to me all the time.

"You're not funny." Iggy spun around and headed to his heating pad.

I swiveled back to Rihanna. "You were about to tell us why Dominic is no longer leading the suspect list."

"Right. As I was about to turn into the sitting room, I could see through an open slit between Mrs. Tully's door and her room where she was doing some hand sewing. I thought this would give me a chance to butter her up by saying I loved to sew."

"You sew?"

"Ah…no, but it wasn't as if she was going to ask for a demonstration of my talents."

My cousin has a point. "What did you learn?"

"She was repairing a coat since its lining had ripped."

Iggy waddled off his pad. "It wasn't ripped. She made a hole."

We all spun toward him. "What are you saying?"

"After the mess with the tea, I decided to check out what Mrs. Tully's been doing," Iggy said.

I held up a hand. "Hold it. What mess with the tea?"

"I was getting to that," Rihanna said. "Let me finish, and then, Iggy, you can tell us what you learned."

"My story is better."

If he had some big news, he would have blurted it out right away. "Rihanna needs to finish."

He lifted his head. "Fine."

"As we were chatting about the coat, I sensed a lot of anxiety and fear."

"Coming from Mrs. Tully?" Jaxson asked.

"Yes. She asked if I'd help her make some tea."

"Help her how? I would imagine she's been making tea by herself for a long time." Something must have prompted her to ask Rihanna. "She might have wanted the company."

"That's what I thought."

"I assume you followed her into the kitchen?"

"I did. She boiled the water and then poured it into the cup. Here's the strange part. Mrs. Tully went over to the cabinet where she keeps the teabags. I didn't think anything of it until she asked that I get the spoons in the drawer." Rihanna rolled her eyes. "It wasn't like she needed my help for that, right? When my back was to her, she must have added the poison to my drink."

"What?" I nearly shouted.

"I read her mind loud and clear. She could tell I knew something and couldn't afford to have me live."

"Are you saying Mrs. Tully tried to kill you?" Jaxson asked.

"Yes. It's why after I carried my cup back to the drawing room, I accidentally on purpose knocked the tea cup over."

"That was the sound Iggy heard," I said mostly to myself.

Iggy crawled up on the coffee table that sat between us. "And that's when I went downstairs and found the coat she was fixing."

I picked him up and held him. I figured he just wanted the attention. "Rihanna, what did Mrs. Tully do?"

"She cleaned it up. I helped her, but I was able to get some of the affected tea on my fingers so it could be tested. It's why I didn't dry my hands. I didn't want anything to rub it off."

That was smart. "You're sure the tea was poisoned?"

"Yes, I'm sure. Mrs. Tully was rather upset that I didn't drink it."

Not much was making sense to me. "Tell me again why she wanted you dead."

Rihanna smiled and turned to Iggy. "Would you like to finish the story, Detective Iggy?"

"Finally. Yes. I checked out her coat and guess what?" He lifted his head.

"Why does everyone want to play guessing games with me? I'm terrible at them." I couldn't help but grunt.

I'm sure it was my imagination, but I swear he rolled his eyes like Rihanna had. "Fine," Iggy said. "The hem of her coat was full of diamonds."

"Diamonds? You're saying that Mrs. Tully found the diamonds and was hiding them?" Though it was clear that was exactly what she was doing.

"Yes. She thought I'd figured out her scam and wanted to shut me up," Rihanna said.

"Shut you up to stop you from saying what? That the diamonds belonged to her in the first place?" I offered. "There's nothing for you to tell."

"Maybe she killed Dr. Hamstead to get them," Iggy said.

"It's possible, but do you have any proof?" I was being quite serious.

"No, but if she tried to kill Rihanna, it's not a stretch," my familiar said.

I looked over at Jaxson. "You've been quiet. What do you think?"

"The diamonds in and of themselves do not imply guilt,

but trying to kill Rihanna is a felony." He took a deep breath. "Maybe the sheriff knows of a way to get the dried tea off Rihanna's fingers and compare it to the poison found in the rum bottle. If the poisons match, it would go a long way to prove Mrs. Tully killed Dr. Hamstead."

"It's worth a try. Are you okay with returning to town?" I asked Rihanna.

"Of course."

Out of habit, I reached for my magical pink diamond necklace, only I'd forgotten it wasn't there.

"Where's your necklace?" Rihanna asked.

"It didn't make it in the process of time traveling."

"I'm sure you'll get it back as soon as we return to the twenty-first century," Jaxson said. "Your grandmother hadn't given it to you in 1972, because you hadn't been born yet."

"I hope you are right." Instead of worrying about it, I needed to deal with the task at hand. There was no reason for Iggy to come with us, because the sheriff would never believe my familiar was so smart. This time Iggy didn't argue when I told him to stay put, but in case he changed his mind, I made sure to lock the door on our way out. I didn't need him trying to solve this case on his own and be harmed in the process.

Not wanting to be stopped by anyone as we left the B&B, the three of us hurried toward the front door. The deputy who had been assigned to ask where we were going hadn't shown up today, something I found strange indeed.

"Where are you headed?" Mrs. Tully asked. It was as if she'd appeared out of thin air. Darn. Caught. Sneaky old lady.

I didn't move until I'd willed my rapid pulse to slow.

Jaxson's hand found my back. "Glinda is hungry. We're

going to find some food."

That comment was never far from the truth. Mrs. Tully smiled. "Have fun."

I had the sense she was happy we'd be out of the house. It would give her the chance to run. If I were her, I'd get out of town quickly.

As soon as we were out of sight from any of the B&B windows, I turned around. "Maybe one of us should stay and see if Mrs. Tully tries to leave town."

"We have time. She probably wasn't expecting to be found out so soon," Jaxson said. "If she plans to leave, it will take her time to pack her things. Personally, I'm not even sure she's positive we know anything—or should I say able to prove anything. She'll never think a teenager is smart enough to get a sample of the poisoned tea on her hands."

"Maybe, but she knows we're on to her," Rihanna said. "Trust me."

I believed my cousin. "Then we better hurry."

With purpose, we strode downtown and marched into the sheriff's office. "We have some information about the Hamstead murder," I announced with as much authority as I could muster.

The officer at the desk studied us. "Weren't you just in here?"

"Yes." I didn't feel the need to defend our presence, however.

"I'll see if the sheriff is in."

Surely, he knew, but he went through the show of making the call. When the officer finished the conversation, he looked up at us. "The sheriff will be right out."

We could have found our way to his office, but I had to remember this wasn't Witch's Cove. Several minutes later, the sheriff came out. His brows rose, but he didn't ask why we were there again. "Come on back to the office."

We'd discussed what we would say. All of us agreed that we needed to leave Iggy out of it. The sheriff wouldn't believe us anyway.

"My officer said you had new information?"

Rihanna sat up straighter. "I saw Mrs. Tully sew diamonds into the lining of her coat."

"And you think these are the diamonds that have been missing for thirty years?" he asked with no surprise in his voice.

"I can't be one hundred percent certain, but there's another reason why I'm here," Rihanna said.

The sheriff studied us. "What is that?"

"Mrs. Tully tried to poison me."

"Uh-huh." He jotted down the information on a yellow note pad. Oh, my. Maybe Sheriff Filmore and Steve Rocker were related. "You don't look ill," he finally said.

"That's because I accidentally tipped over the cup. Mrs. Tully was quite upset that I didn't drink it."

"Why would she try to poison you?"

"I didn't ask her, but if I had to guess, I'd say it was because she saw me watching her hide her diamonds in the lining of her coat. Is that the action of an innocent woman?" Rihanna asked. "Perhaps her guilt over murdering Dr. Hamstead made her want to get rid of a witness."

I was so impressed with my cousin. I'm not sure I would have remained so calm.

"Let's suppose what you say is true," the sheriff said. "Can you prove she tried to kill you?"

"I'm hoping *you* can," Rihanna said. "I made sure to get some tea on my hands. While they are dry, I've not washed them. Is there any way you can test them for poison? It might be the same kind used to kill Dr. Hamstead."

The sheriff huffed. Maybe she had impressed him. "I'll call our lab and see how they want to handle this. If you wouldn't mind waiting in the lobby, I'll let you know what I find out."

It wasn't as if we had a choice. "Sure."

The three of us returned to the sitting area. While the warmth I experienced in Witch's Cove was far greater than this sheriff's office, at least he didn't dismiss our claim.

It was over an hour before someone came to test Rihanna's hands. They escorted her somewhere and said it wouldn't be long before she returned, but that was a lie. She didn't show up for about ninety minutes.

"What took you so long?" I asked as she dropped down next to me.

"They had to keep redoing the test."

I was surprised they weren't more sophisticated in the 70's. "Did they say if we could leave?" I asked. "Iggy will be upset that we've been gone so long. Not to mention, Mrs. Tully will have had plenty of time to pack and make arrangements to leave."

She shrugged. "They didn't say we couldn't."

"Good." Just as we stood, three people we knew walked through the door. I just didn't expect to see one of them in handcuffs.

Chapter Fifteen

MRS. TULLY, STEPHANIE Carlton, and Dominic Geno walked in. At one point in time, all were suspects in Dr. Hamstead's murder, though Jaxson, Rihanna, and I believed Mrs. Tully was the true murderer. If nothing else, trying to poison Rihanna should be enough to punish her—assuming the tea was tainted. That conclusion, of course, was based solely on Rihanna's ability to read Mrs. Tully's mind.

"What are you doing here?" I asked no one in particular.

"If you will take a seat for a few minutes, I'll return to explain," Dominic said.

Explain? What could a PhD student explain to us? And why was he escorting Mrs. Tully in handcuffs? Even more confusing was why Stephanie was with them. We must be in an episode of the *Twilight Zone*. Any minute, I expected to wake up and find myself back in the office kissing Jaxson. Sure, that was a fantasy, but I had no better explanation.

We returned to our seats just as he'd instructed, with Rihanna on one side of me and Jaxson on the other. "What am I missing?" I asked, even though I doubted they had any idea either.

"Looks like Mrs. Tully has been caught," Jaxson said.

"I could understand if she'd been escorted by an officer of

the law, but what were those two doing with her?"

It would be another twenty minutes before we learned the answer to that question.

Stephanie was the first one to come out. She sat next to us. "I bet you have some questions."

"Some?" was all I could say for a few seconds. "What's going on?"

"For starters, my name really is Stephanie Carlton. I do have a daughter who lives here, and I did attend Charlotte College. Everything else was a lie." She held up a hand. "I'm an FBI agent, here with Dominic Geno, to uncover a ring of thieves who prey on people like Mrs. Tully. Dr. Hamstead was but a small cog in the wheel, however."

I was speechless for once in my life. I never considered she wasn't who she said she was.

"Did you have three husbands?" Jaxson asked.

She chuckled. "That's what you want to know? The answer is no. I had one, and we divorced years ago. My job is mainly in Washington D.C., and Tom couldn't deal with me working all of the time."

"Does your daughter know?" I finally asked.

"Yes, which is one reason why she and her family are on a cruise, though they often go on one over Christmas. As much as it would have been great to see them, my job can be dangerous, and I always feel better if they aren't around."

My head was spinning. And here I thought we'd figured everything out. Clearly, I couldn't have been more wrong. I should chalk it up to time travel, right?

"Did they take a long time to test my hands so the sheriff could have you search Mrs. Tully's stuff?" Rihanna asked.

"Yes. We asked him to stall. Having you three return would have put the case in jeopardy."

Who knew? "What happened when the sheriff arrested you before? Did you have to tell him the truth?"

"I did. I never expected someone to murder Michael," she said. "Thankfully, a quick call to my supervisor assured the sheriff I was who I claimed to be. He had to let me go once he understood what was at stake."

"What about Phil?" I asked.

"He was an innocent bystander—or so we believe at this moment. Dom has a degree in physics, so he was the perfect person to pretend to be some PhD student."

"Was Dr. Hamstead a real professor?" Rihanna asked.

"He was. It gave him a good cover story for visiting college towns. He often would travel from school to school once he found out which widow in the area might have something of value."

This was wild. "Have you been onto him for a while then?"

"Dom has been. He's been keeping a careful watch on Dr. Hamstead for about four months now. I guess you could say we got lucky that Mrs. Tully killed him."

"Lucky?"

"I should have said, unlucky in that he can't provide us with any information about who he worked for, but lucky in that his death saves the taxpayers a long trial."

They still would have to try Mrs. Tully, though her case might be more open and shut.

"I have to say, you had us fooled." I didn't think it appropriate to mention that Rihanna thought Stephanie had been hiding something all along.

"I'm glad to know that."

"What's next for you?" Jaxson asked.

"I'm not sure. I just started working for the Bureau. In fact, this is actually my first case. Before that, I was a cop for over twenty years. Being with mostly all men has been quite stressful, so right now, I'm weighing my options. I might even retire. I would really like to settle down here and get to know my daughter and grandkids again."

What a great sentiment. Before I could comment further, Dominic came out.

He looked over at us and smiled. "I trust Stephanie has filled you in?"

"She has."

"I have to hand it to you, Glinda. When you asked me about the details of the computer program I was working on, I thought my cover was going to be blown. How did you learn about Fortran? It's only been around for about fifteen years."

Yikes. I certainly couldn't say that most people in the math and physics field knew a smattering of Fortran, though, I personally started with Basic. "It's a hobby of mine."

"I see. Keep it up. I think computers will become very important in the future," Dominic said.

He had no idea. "I agree." I held up a finger. "One more question. If they prove that Mrs. Tully killed Dr. Hamstead and tried to poison Rihanna, she'll obviously go to prison. What happens to the diamonds since she has no relatives?"

"I'm no estate lawyer, so I couldn't say. The Ashton B&B is on the Preservation Society list of homes. Some of the diamonds might be sold to fix it up."

It needed it. "Will they find someone to run it?" I asked.

"Let's hope they do."

Once we said our goodbyes, the three of us left. *Brr.* The outside air seemed colder than I remembered. "Since we're so close to Madam Criant's place, we should tell her that we helped solve the crime. I mean Rihanna and Iggy helped solve the crime."

My cousin smiled. "We all did our part."

I supposed that was true. The psychic's shop was only a few blocks away, but unfortunately, the inside was dark. Out of habit—and because I was curious—I twisted the door handle. It opened. I spun around. "Do you think she's here?" I asked.

"Peek your head in," Jaxson said.

I did. "Madam Criant? Are you here?"

When she didn't answer, my gut did a little dance. I had no basis for my feeling, but I had the sense something was amiss.

Jaxson placed a hand on my shoulder. "Glinda? What's wrong?"

"I don't know. Something doesn't feel right."

He turned me around to face him. "Talk to me."

I looked over at Rihanna. "What are you feeling?" She was highly intuitive.

"I'm not sure. I know Madam Criant is psychic, but it's not as if she was at the station and saw Mrs. Tully's arrest. I'm a bit surprised she isn't here."

"What do you all make of the fact the front door wasn't locked?"

"It's a small town. She might have forgotten, or else she

didn't see the need. Are you thinking someone broke in and kidnapped our psychic?" Jaxson asked.

"I don't know. Maybe." Acid poured into my stomach. "If that's the case, we are doomed."

My partner in crime gathered me to his chest, and it helped relax me. "We should talk to Evan. He and Madam Criant seemed close. I bet he knows where to find her."

I looked up at him. "You are a wise man, Jaxson Harrison."

He smiled briefly. "I don't know about that, but we should ask him."

The three of us trudged through the town and then up that big hill that led to the Ashton House B&B. I couldn't help but wonder what was going to happen to the place. Would it close, be sold, or would the town try to renovate it?

Before I could figure anything out, we'd arrived back. Inside, it was eerily quiet. Mrs. Tully was in jail, Dr. Hamstead was dead, and Stephanie and Dominic were probably filling out a ton of paperwork at the sheriff's office. The only ones who might be here were Phil and Evan—and Iggy, of course.

"Let's see if Evan knows something," Jaxson said.

We went to the kitchen, but it was empty. I shouldn't be surprised since his job was only to make breakfast for the B&B. Was he even aware that his boss had been accused of murder? I didn't want to think he was involved in any way.

I turned to Rihanna and Jaxson. "Any ideas?"

"I bet either Sheila or Sissy would know how to contact Evan, or we could just wait until tomorrow morning when he shows up to work to ask him," he said.

"I say we rest a bit, and then head downtown to the diner," Rihanna suggested.

My cousin had good ideas. "You always are the logical one."

With that settled, we went upstairs to regroup. Learning that we'd all been fooled didn't settle well with me, but I had to remember we were dealing with professionals who would uncover the truth. "I have a feeling that your father was like Dominic and Stephanie," I said to Rihanna.

"He'd have to have been good to survive so long in the business." She removed her jacket. "If you don't mind, I'm going to soak in a hot tub."

"That sounds divine. Go for it."

All of this must be quite stressful for a teenager, though at times, Rihanna seemed better at handling things than I was.

Needing time to think, I dropped down onto the bed. Iggy crawled up next to me. "What's up?" he asked.

"You won't believe what happened." I proceeded to fill him in, and he only asked a few questions.

"The case is solved then?" he asked.

"Thanks to you, it is."

"Can we go home now?" The hope in his voice tore at me.

"As soon as we find Madam Criant." It was painful to explain how we were unable to locate her.

"Maybe people don't lock their doors like they do in our time," Iggy said.

"Let's hope you are right."

I must have been more tired than I thought, because I fell asleep. I only awoke when Rihanna shook my shoulder. "Do you want to eat?" she asked.

"I do, but I dread going out in the cold again."

"I doubt they have Uber Eats yet, and home delivery might not be a thing yet, either."

"Fine. I'll get ready."

By the time we finished layering to go out, it was a little after six. When we knocked on Jaxson's door, he opened up and smiled. Just seeing his face helped keep me centered. "Ready?"

"Let's do this."

"I suppose we could invite Phil to join us, but it might be difficult to get the scoop on Madam Criant with him in tow." I never liked for anyone to be alone for a meal, however.

Jaxson rubbed my back. "He'll be fine. I imagine Dominic will be explaining things to him."

"I hope so."

The trip to town was rather serene. The wind was nonexistent, even though it had started to lightly snow. The streetlights backlit the cascading snowflakes, making it look like magic had come to Charlotte, Ohio.

The big negative was that we hadn't found Madam Criant or Evan Drugan yet. I really hoped those two hadn't run off with each other. Wouldn't that make a mess of things? We needed to find out where they lived and search for them at home. They couldn't have disappeared. Or could they have?

When we arrived at the River Bend Café, I was prepared for disappointment. Luck, however, decided to shine on us. Sissy was there, along with another server. While the place was quite full, we were able to snag a booth.

I slid in and almost felt at home. When our friendly gossip queen spotted us, she smiled and waved. A minute later she came over.

"Hey, there. Can you believe they're saying that Mrs. Tully murdered that poor man?" Sissy said, her eyes wide.

Gossip ran wild no matter the time or place, didn't it? I wasn't about to say Mr. Hamstead hadn't been all that innocent. "She's been arrested, but I have no idea if the sheriff has enough proof that she did it."

The problem was that if he couldn't prove she killed Dr. Hamstead, Mrs. Tully might go free, despite having tried to poison Rihanna. Even if the attorney showed a jury the results of Rihanna's poison test, if she wasn't present in court to tell her side of the story, the case might be dismissed.

"Personally, I always thought Mrs. Tully was more sad than angry," Sissy said.

"How so?"

Chapter Sixteen

"JOSEPHINE TULLY USED to be so sweet," Sissy said.

"Until her husband died, I'm guessing?" That seemed to be a theme around here.

"It took a few years for her to realize her loss, but yes."

"Did you ever think she was capable of murder?" Jaxson asked.

"Never. I think times have been hard—on all of us really. I heard she'd received a notice the bank might foreclose on her property."

Sympathy swamped me. "She was desperate for money."

Sissy nodded. Several more people piled into the diner. "I'd love to stay and chat, but…"

"I understand."

"What can I get you?"

I rattled off my go-to request of a grilled cheese sandwich with tomato, some fries, and a sweet tea. Jaxson ordered fish and Rihanna a hamburger.

Sissy left, and I was finally able to let down my guard. Being out of the B&B seemed to help. "Our plan is to ask Evan tomorrow where Madam Criant is, and then go home to Witch's Cove." I liked how upbeat I sounded.

"What if she only told us she could return us to our time

in order to get our help with the murder?" Rihanna asked.

"I prefer not to worry about something like that just yet." Sheesh. My cousin wasn't normally so negative. So what if I'd been that way earlier?

"We need a backup plan," Jaxson said.

He was right. As usual. "Okay, in case Evan doesn't know where Madam Criant is, we'll ask Sissy if she knows if our resident psychic has any relatives in town."

He nodded. "Sounds good. If that fails, Sissy might know how to find out where Madam Criant lives."

"Excellent." The other server delivered our drinks. I had to admit that having a plan was a relief. "What is the first thing you are going to do when we get home?" I asked my cousin.

Rihanna sipped her soda. "Call Gavin and tell him I'm safe."

I blew out a breath. "I can't imagine the panic that our town is in right now with three of its citizens missing—or four if you count Iggy. Aunt Fern will have everyone searching the whole county."

"All the more reason to get back to Witch's Cove as fast as we can," Jaxson said.

"Amen."

A few minutes later, Sissy delivered our food. "By any chance do you know Bethany Criant?" I asked.

"The psychic?"

"Yes."

"In name only," Sissy said.

Darn. "It's kind of important that we talk to her. Do you think you could ask around to find out if she has any relatives in town or where she lives?"

"Sure, but her fiancé works at the B&B. Why not ask him?"

Her fiancé? "Evan Drugan?"

"That's him, but I think they left already."

My stomach flipped. "Left for where?"

Sissy shrugged. "Mind you this is hearsay, but I think they flew to the Bahamas to get married."

Okay, that was the last straw. Why in the world would Madam Criant claim she could help us if she had no intention of doing so? "Wow. I didn't see that coming. Thanks."

Sissy smiled. "You bet." She then returned to serve some other tables.

"What do you think that means?" I asked.

Jaxson huffed. "She might have asked us to help solve the murder, because she wondered if Evan had been involved in the heist. She wanted the assurance that he wasn't."

Rihanna set down her drink. "Would a person really marry someone if they thought their fiancé was capable of theft or worse murder?"

"I sure wouldn't."

Rihanna raised her brows. "Then why ask for our help?"

"I don't know, but if she was a fake, we need to find another way to get home."

Jaxson chuckled. "Glinda Goodall, the eternal optimist. I love it."

"I'll be more optimistic if I can come up with a plan."

"I'm sure you will."

With my hopes of getting back to Witch's Cove fading, my appetite wasn't the best. Because of that, for the remainder of the meal, I was rather quiet.

After we paid, we headed back to the rather empty B&B. To my surprise, both Dominic and Stephanie were there, sitting together by the fire.

I turned to Rihanna and Jaxson. "Do you mind if I stop and chat with them for a second?"

"No problem." Jaxson stroked my cheek and then walked upstairs behind Rihanna.

Both Stephanie and Dominic turned around. "Why so glum?" Stephanie asked.

I was bad at hiding my feelings. "I'm not sure. Please tell me the sheriff has enough evidence to put Mrs. Tully away."

They both nodded. "Don't worry about that. She admitted she poisoned Dr. Hamstead because he refused to give back her diamonds. He'd threatened her, saying that if she told anyone about his find, he'd kill her."

"Will she claim self-defense?" I wasn't sure a threat like that counted as self-defense, though. I really should take a few courses in law enforcement when I returned home.

"I don't know. All she kept saying was that she didn't do anything wrong since he was a thief and that he needed to be punished. I'm not sure she cared that he threatened her. While she was correct that Dr. Hamstead was a thief, killing him wasn't the answer."

"No, it wasn't, but I hope the jury takes the threat into consideration. I think she was still grieving over the loss of her husband. With her home in financial trouble, she was probably at her wits end."

"That's not a reason to kill someone," Dominic said.

"I know. With the case more or less solved will you both

be able to go home, or do you have to stay through the trial?" I asked.

"I'll be heading back to D.C.," Dominic said. "If I'm needed here, I'll return."

"How did Phil react to all of this?" I asked.

"He took it hard."

"I bet. He lost who he thought was a mentor as well as you as a friend."

Dominic nodded. "And you? Will you and your friends be heading back to Witch's Cove?"

For a second I'd forgotten that I'd said I was from there, though he'd think I'd meant Witch's Cove circa 1972. "Yes. Sooner rather than later." I turned to Stephanie. "Have you made any final decisions about your future?"

"Not yet. My daughter gets back from her cruise in a few days, and I want to pass it by her first. It's possible the idea of her mother living in the same town will be a terrible one."

I shook my head. "I'm sure she'll love it."

"I hope so."

I didn't want to keep Jaxson and Rihanna waiting. "I'm heading upstairs. I'll see you both tomorrow."

When I entered, Rihanna was there with Iggy who was sitting on his heating pad playing with something. Jaxson must have gone back to his room. "What do you have there, buddy?"

"A coin."

A coin was what started this whole mess in the first place. I knelt in front of him. "May I see it?"

"Sure."

As I studied it, my pulse rose. "This looks just like the one

I made a wish on when I was back at the Tiki Hut."

Rihanna came over. "May I?"

I handed it to her. She flipped it over. "It's not real. It's too light."

"The one I made the wish on wasn't real either. Jaxson thought it probably came from some parade float." I turned back to Iggy. "Where did you get this?"

"It was next to my heating pad."

"Any idea how it got there?"

"No," he said.

I believed him. "Maybe the maid dropped it."

"Why don't you make another wish?" Iggy said.

"I guess it wouldn't hurt." I looked up at my cousin. "How about asking Jaxson to come in here in case this works?"

She smiled. "Sure."

Rihanna ran out and the two returned seconds later. Jaxson rushed over to me. "Is it the same coin?"

"No. I left the one I found in our office, but this looks eerily similar."

"Time travel does strange things to our minds," he said.

"You got that right."

"Make a wish," he urged.

"I can't imagine it working, but hey, maybe it will."

Rihanna joined us so that all four of us were in close proximity to each other. "I want to replicate exactly what I did the first time. I'll close my eyes and say my wish out loud. Then, I'll kiss Jaxson."

"You need the mistletoe," Iggy said.

"It can't hurt." The mistletoe was half gone, but I was

game.

Rihanna carried it over and handed it to me. It made sense to keep things as close to the same as before.

"Here goes." I closed my eyes. "I wish that I was back in Witch's Cove with Jaxson, Rihanna, and Iggy in 2020." I hope it wasn't 2021 by now. I inhaled and held the mistletoe above Jaxson's head. He bent down and delivered a wonderful kiss.

Suddenly, a bright light swirled around me, and I swear I was falling, just like the last time. I thought it was the effect of the kiss until everything stopped—sound, the air around me, and my heart. When I opened my eyes, I was back in our office!

"I did it." I spun around. "Jaxson? Rihanna? Where are you? Iggy, are you hiding?" When no one answered my throat almost closed up.

With my heart beating way too hard, I couldn't think. I had to sit down and collect my thoughts. Surely, I wasn't the only one who made it. The others had to be here. But where? Think?

I jumped up and grabbed my purse. Inside was my phone. When I looked at the date, I sighed a big breath of relief. It was still Christmas Eve. That meant this whole thing had been a dream. Right?

I immediately called Jaxson's number, but it went to voicemail. "Hi, it's me. I know this will sound weird, but could you call me back after you get this message? Something really strange happened to me, and I need to be sure I'm not losing my mind."

After I disconnected, I walked over to my computer and

typed in Charlotte, Ohio. While it loaded, I feared there was no such town, but when it popped up, I pumped my fist and then did a quick search. Sure enough, there was a college there, and the town was located on the Ohio River. As much as I wanted to see if there was an Ashton B&B, I thought it best if I headed back to my apartment to find Iggy. Surely, he would be there, or with Aimee.

Happy that things were getting back to normal, I took the outside staircase. I could have asked Drake if he knew where his brother was, but I wasn't ready for the long explanation for why I was worried. When I entered my apartment, I expected to see Iggy on his stool. Only he wasn't there.

"Iggy? I need to talk to you."

I slipped into the kitchen thinking he might be in there, only he wasn't. I refused to believe that my trip back in time was real. It couldn't be. If it were, it might mean I'd never see Jaxson, Rihanna, or Iggy ever again, and that was totally unacceptable.

Wanting to check my aunt's apartment for Iggy, I stepped across the hallway and knocked, but no one answered. Only then did I remember she was going to be with her friends this afternoon.

"Aimee, are you in there?"

A few seconds later, my aunt's cat crawled out of the cat door. "Hey, Glinda."

At least something was as it should be. "Have you seen Iggy?"

"I saw him this morning."

At first, I was excited, until I realize that in theory, I had been here the morning of Christmas Eve, too. "Not in the last hour?"

"No."

"Okay, thanks."

If no one was at the office or here, and Jaxson wasn't answering his phone, I clearly needed help. I wasn't sure if my mother could assist me, but she might be able to explain what happened.

Chapter Seventeen

WITHOUT WASTING ANY more time, I rushed over to the mortuary. My parents were going to be by themselves this evening, so it wasn't as if I would be interrupting anything.

I ran up the steps and knocked. My mother answered a few seconds later. Naturally, Toto barked up a storm.

"Glinda, what's wrong? I thought you'd be with Jaxson."

"About that. Can I come in?"

"Of course, sweetie." She moved to the side. "Let me get you some tea and we'll talk."

"How about a glass of wine instead?"

"Oh, my. Did you and Jaxson break up?"

I huffed out a laugh. "I wish it were that simple. No."

"Do you want me to get your dad?"

My father had his faults, but he was good at keeping his cool. "I'd like that."

My mother fixed my drink and handed it to me. "Stan? Glinda's here," she called. When he didn't answer, she went in search of him.

While she tried to locate him, I went into the dining room and sat at the table. I don't know why I thought that spot was more appropriate than the more comfortable living room.

Both of my parents found me and sat across from me. "Tell us what happened?" my mother said.

"What I'm about to tell you will sound absolutely crazy, but I can assure you all of it is true—at least I believe it to be true."

"We're listening."

I started with finding the coin, about making the wish to see snow, and then kissing Jaxson with the mistletoe. "When I opened my eyes, all of us—Iggy included—had been transported back fifty years to a town in Ohio."

"Ohio?" my father asked. "Why there?"

That was his first question? "I don't have any idea, but are you saying you believe that we actually time traveled?"

He leaned back in his chair. "If I can turn into a werewolf, then anything is possible."

Wow. I hadn't expected that response.

"Tell us everything," my mother urged.

I told them about landing in the lobby of the Ashton B&B, and then how one of the guests was murdered.

"Another murder? Oh, Glinda," my mom said. "Why are you always involved in those?"

"I didn't ask for it."

She waved a hand. "Go on."

I explained about Madam Criant and how she'd said all we had to do was solve the murder, and then she'd help us get back to our time. "Only when we went to find her, she'd apparently run off to the Bahamas and gotten married."

"How did you get back here then if you never found her?" Dad asked.

I told them about the coin appearing by Iggy's side. "Here's the thing. Only I returned. Jaxson, Rihanna, and Iggy are still stuck back in 1972—or I think they are, since I can't find Rhianna or Iggy anywhere, and Jaxson doesn't answer his phone."

"How do you think we can help?" Mom asked.

"I don't know. I'm at a loss. I thought about going back in time, but even if I wanted to teleport back, I don't have the coin anymore."

Mom looked over at Dad. "What do you think, Stan?"

"She'll need someone more powerful than us."

That meant either Gertrude Poole or her grandson Levy. His coven seemed to be quite powerful. One of them might know something about time travel. "I'll give it a try. I know Gertrude is with Aunt Fern, but maybe Levy is free."

"You said you were there for days and yet no time seemed to have passed here," my mother said.

"Yes, and I can't explain it, but I appreciate you not telling me I am crazy."

"We'd never do that."

Something was going on with them, but I couldn't figure it out. "Have you ever heard of this happening to anyone before?" I hadn't expected them to be so calm.

Once more my parents looked at each other. What I wouldn't give to have Rihanna here. She could read their minds.

"Maybe, but it doesn't sound like the same thing. Talk to Levy and let us know what he says. I really hope we can have Christmas together tomorrow."

I sucked in a breath. "Oh, no. Rihanna is supposed to go

out with Gavin tonight. He'll be beside himself if she doesn't show."

My mother looked at her watch. "It's only four. When were they to meet?"

"I think seven. He was going to take her out to dinner in Ocean View."

"Maybe you should give him a call."

"Do you think a nineteen-year old will believe me? It took a lot to convince his mother that magic exists. She's a scientist, as is her son."

"You could make up a story, but they won't believe you. You're a terrible liar."

I laughed. "That is true. Once Rihanna returns, she'll tell him the truth. Whether he believes her or not is not under my control. I might as well let him know that his date might not arrive."

"Good luck, sweetie."

I would have stayed longer, but I needed to get ahold of Levy Poole. Then I'd talk to Gavin Sanchez and try to explain time travel, though I think I'd have better luck teaching calculus to my seventh graders.

I returned to the office just in case one of the three figured out how to time travel back to Witch's Cove, but the office was eerily empty. I sat there drumming my fingers for at least fifteen minutes, waiting anxiously for them to appear. Eventually, I couldn't handle being idle. Since Levy was my best hope, I called him.

"Glinda?" Why did he sound worried? Did he know something?

"Yes, it's me. I'm really sorry to disturb you, but I've been through a life-altering event and need some help." That might have been a bit dramatic, but it would definitely be life-altering if I lost my familiar, my boyfriend, and my cousin all at once. Not that they would be dead, but I'd never see them again.

"Tell me what happened."

I explained about the coin, the wish, and then the traveling back in time. "I thought we were there for days, but no time had passed here."

"I've never heard of anything like that before."

I wasn't surprised. "The worst thing was that Madam Criant, a local psychic, claimed to be able to help us."

"Madam Criant?"

My chest squeezed tight. "Yes." There was no way he'd know her. "Why?"

"My grandmother used to know a woman by the name of Bethany Criant who was a psychic. My grandmother and she kept in touch for years."

I mentally did the math. If Madam Criant was forty, like I suspected, then she'd be ninety now. I walked over to the sofa and sat down. I wasn't sure my legs could support me. "Is she still alive?"

"I believe she passed two years ago, but call my grandmother. If this woman claimed she could help you, Grandma might be able to contact her."

Disturbing her when she was with friends might not be cool, but I didn't want Jaxson, Rihanna, and Iggy to wonder if I was even alive. "So, you have no idea how time travel works?"

"Not the faintest idea, nor has anyone in my coven ever

mentioned it's possible."

If my mom couldn't help, and Levy's coven was powerless, I was left with one choice. "I'll contact Gertrude. Thank you."

"Good luck. If anyone can do this, you can."

I swallowed a laugh. "Rihanna maybe, but me?"

"Glinda, you need to have some faith."

He sounded like my grandmother. At the thought of how much she'd helped me in the past, I reached for my pink pendant that had been missing ever since my time travel. To my delight, it was securely hanging around my neck. "I will."

As soon as I disconnected, I called Aunt Fern.

"Glinda? Is something wrong?"

Her greeting implied I'd interrupted a good time. "Yes, I'm sorry. Can I come over?"

"I'm at Miriam's."

"I know, but I need everyone's help." That might not be technically true, but if Gertrude wanted to have a séance to contact Madam Criant, I figured the more people involved the better. Not only that, I figured it would be better for the gossip queens to hear my side of the story and not get some hand-me-down version from my aunt.

"Give me a second."

She must have covered the speaker on her phone because I only heard mumblings. "Of course. Come over now. Will Jaxson be with you?"

"No. He's missing. As is Iggy and Rihanna. It's why I need your help."

She sucked in a shuddering breath. "Did you tell the sheriff?"

"I'm afraid only Gertrude can truly help."

She didn't say anything for a moment. "Come quickly."

Not wanting to delay further, I grabbed my jacket and tore down the stairs. These women would ask a million questions, but I hoped that Gertrude could ask them to delay the inquisition until my friends and family had returned.

I didn't want to have to decide between staying in Witch's Cove without them or returning to cold Charlotte, Ohio with no chance of ever seeing my parents or my aunt again.

With that horrible option lodged in my mind, I jumped into my car and took off. Once there, I cut the engine and jogged up to the front door. Noise came from inside, but it sounded like concerned conversation rather than a celebration.

Miriam answered. "Oh, Glinda. Come in."

Clearly, my aunt had alerted everyone to the fact that three people were missing. And yes, Iggy was a person to me. As soon as I spotted Gertrude, the tension in my shoulders let go a bit.

The ladies had a chair ready for me.

"Can I get you something to drink?" Miriam asked.

"How about some iced tea?"

"Coming right up."

My aunt scooted her chair closer and took hold of my hand. "I'm so sorry about Jaxson, Rihanna, and Iggy."

"Levy just called me," Gertrude said. "This involves my college roommate, Bethany Criant?"

Her roommate? That might be the connection I was seeking—not that it would help get my friends back. "I guess. She'd be about your age now, but Levy said she'd passed?"

"Yes, I'm afraid so. Please tell us everything."

To my surprise, the women let me tell them my tale. "I really thought that when Iggy found the coin that we'd all return."

"You're certain it wasn't a dream?" Pearl asked.

"I'm pretty sure. If it were, why aren't the others here?"

No one answered, until Gertrude cleared her throat. "There is only one way to find out."

"What's that?"

"We need to contact Bethany."

I was hoping she'd suggest that. "I'm game."

The group murmured their agreement. Dare I say they seemed quite excited.

Miriam stood. "Let me clear off the dining room table. We can all sit around there. What else do you need?"

"Some candles," Gertrude said. "That's all."

It only took a few minutes to gather the supplies. Everyone sat down. Maybe because I was the one who might end up channeling Madam Criant, I sat between Gertrude and my aunt. Both women had powers. The rest in the room did not.

"Please touch your fingers to the person next to you and don't let go. Also please don't speak. Do you understand, Pearl?" Gertrude asked.

I almost chuckled how well everyone understood the sheriff's grandmother's inclinations.

She did a zippering motion of her mouth.

"Very well," Gertrude said. "Let's begin."

Chapter Eighteen

LIKE I'D HEARD her do before, Gertrude invoked a spirit, but this time of Bethany Criant. I hoped that if she had indeed eloped with Evan Drugan, that she hadn't changed her last name. If Gertrude had been in contact with her former roommate recently, Gertrude would be aware of the name change or lack thereof.

In the past, I had been able to sit back and kind of relax, but not this time. Too much was at stake.

I waited for Madam Criant to speak through Gertrude or even appear as a ghost, but instead, something inside of me vibrated, causing my body to shake. My mouth opened, and it was as if something, or someone, took over my mind.

"A token found will be round. Tap it twice to stop time thrice. To bring them back or join them there, do whichever you so dare," I said—though it sounded like someone else's voice.

The breath left my body, and the next thing I knew, my aunt was whispering in my ear. "Glinda, wake up."

Wake up? I wasn't asleep. Someone grabbed my shoulders to help me sit up. When I opened my eyes, several faces were staring at me. "Hi?" I said, not sure if I was even talking.

"Are you okay?" Aunt Fern asked.

Was I? I looked around the room. "Yes, but I feel a bit…funny."

"Do you remember what you said?" Gertrude asked.

"Only bits and pieces." When I lifted my hand to move the hair out of my face, I spotted a gold coin on the table. "Where did this come from?" I asked.

The women looked at each other and mumbled they didn't know.

"Our fingers were all touching," Gertrude said. "No one could have put it there."

"Madam Criant sent it," I said with confidence.

"But she's dead," Maude said.

"Her spirit sent it then." I looked over at Gertrude, thinking she might know.

"Anything is possible in the spirit world. I'll be the first to admit that time travel is not my area of expertise."

I picked it up, and the second I touched it, my memory rushed back about what Bethany Criant had said. "This is the key to getting them back."

"Are you going to tap it twice then?" my aunt asked.

"Yes. Why wouldn't I?" I thought it was a no-brainer.

"What if it sends you back in time?" Dolly asked.

I stilled. "Naturally, I will concentrate on them coming here."

"How does the coin know which of the two options you want if you merely tap it twice?" she asked.

"That's an excellent question. I'll wish with all my might that Jaxson, Rihanna, and Iggy come back to our time. It's that simple." Or so I wanted to believe.

"But what if you end up back there?" Maude asked.

"I can't leave them," I blurted. I turned to my aunt. "Please tell my parents what happened if I suddenly disappear. And let Gavin know, too, though I don't think he'll believe you."

"Are you sure?" My aunt clasped my hand, leaned over, and hugged me.

I worked hard not to cry. This would be the biggest decision in my life. "Yes. I'm sure. Being without all of you would be horrific but being without them would be worse."

Gertrude nodded. "So be it. Hold the coin in your palm and tap it twice then."

Now that I literally held the future in my hand, I was having some guilt. Was I being selfish? No. A life without those three would be no life at all. Before I chickened out, I tapped the coin. "We will try to return as soon as we can, assuming I end up there again."

I performed the ritual, but when I opened my eyes, I expected to see Jaxson and Rihanna standing in front of us, but all I saw were my aunt and her friends.

"Oh. I guess it didn't work." I worked hard not to sound as disappointed as I felt.

My cell rang, and my heart skipped a beat. Who would be calling me? Could it be Levy to see if I'd found a solution? I leaned over, grabbed my purse, and retrieved my phone. When I saw it was Jaxson, tears welled in my eyes.

"Are you back?" I asked, my tongue sticking to the roof of my mouth.

"Yes, we are. Where are you?"

I laughed. "I can't believe it. It worked." I literally bounced up and down in my chair. "I'm with Gertrude, Aunt

Fern, and the others. We did a séance in the hopes of finding out how to get you back."

All of the women were grinning, too.

"I wasn't sure it was real, but maybe it was," Jaxson said.

"Trust me, it was. I'll be right there." I disconnected. I suppose I should stay and tell these wonderful ladies more, but I had to see for myself that my friends were back. "I've got to go. And thank you."

"No, thank you!" Miriam said. "This is the best Christmas Eve we've ever had.

I quickly hugged my aunt, grabbed my jacket, and rushed out. Oh, darn. I forgot to ask if they were at the office or somewhere else, but I would start at the office.

Careful not to crash on the way back to town, I didn't let my gaze wander even once. As soon as I arrived, I raced up the stairs and burst into the office. There, I was greeted with the most joyous sight. I didn't know who I should hug first, but the choice was taken from me when Jaxson rushed up to me.

He clasped my face, leaned down, and kissed me. For a split second, I feared we'd all time travel back to Ohio again. With my heart beating way too hard, I wrapped my arms around him, never wanting to be separated again.

Jaxson broke the kiss. "I really thought I'd lost you," he said, desperation tearing at his voice.

"You? I've been going crazy looking for all of you. I truly thought I'd never see any of you again." I blinked so as not to let any tears fall.

He stepped back and let Rihanna hug me. My cousin either had time to change, or she, too, had been returned wearing her twenty-first century clothes.

I looked around. "Where's Iggy?"

When no one said anything, my stomach churned. A second later, my familiar crawled out from under the sofa. "You looking for me?"

I swear he sounded like Al Pacino who'd delivered that famous line. "Yes." I knelt down, lifted him up, and tried not to hold him too tightly.

When I caught my breath, I stood. "Tell me everything."

"I'll get us something to drink," Rihanna said.

"It's like old times. I will never take anything for granted again," I said.

"Me neither." Jaxson slipped his phone from his pocket and stroked it. "I sure missed modern technology."

"Amen." With our drinks in hand, we all took a seat on the sofa. Even Iggy crawled onto my lap. "Tell me everything," I said.

"First off, I can't believe no time has passed," Jaxson said.

I looked over at Rihanna. "She called it."

"I was just making it up." Her eyes widened. "Speaking of time, I need to get ready. Gavin will be here in thirty minutes."

"Go. We can catch up later." I looked over at Jaxson.

"After you disappeared, we were frantic. We looked everywhere for you. Rihanna was convinced you'd returned since you vanished right in front of our eyes. I finally had to believe you were here and safe. The alternative was too horrible."

"I felt the same way."

"Even worse was that we had to wait five more days until Madam Criant returned from her honeymoon. She apologized, of course, but she said she was waiting for a friend to contact her."

"A friend? That might have been Gertrude." I briefly told him they were college roommates and that we'd held a séance to find out what we had to do to get you back.

"I had no idea."

"How would you? What did you have to do for her to send you back—or wasn't she the one to help you?"

He blew out a breath. "She was. At first, I thought her whole psychic thing might have been a scam, but then I figured we had nothing to lose. Madam Criant merely asked that I give her the best three stock investments so that her children would have a chance at a good life."

"Really? What did you tell her?"

He smiled. "I said Apple, Amazon, and Google."

"Did she ask what a fruit and a river had to do with wealth?"

He laughed. "More or less. I told her they had something to do with computers. She wrote the names down in the hopes future generations would understand their value."

"Smart. I wonder if she really believed you."

"I think she did, but she was skeptical, so I told her to invest in IBM. At least that company was around back then. I actually checked and found the stock market was a little under a thousand at the time."

I whistled. "Wow. Talk about inflation."

"I know."

"Once you gave her the keys to the kingdom, then what?" I asked.

She told me to hold some gold coin, tap it twice, and then boom. We were back.

The coincidence was too hard to believe, but I also couldn't ignore it. I told him what I went through. "I thought that I brought you back."

"Maybe both had to work at the same time," he said.

I drank my tea. I was suddenly parched for the taste of it. "I, for one, don't care how you got back here. All that matters is that you are back."

"I couldn't agree more."

My ever-curious mind refused to stop working. "If you were gone for five more days, did you learn anything else?"

"Just that after the sheriff's department did a thorough search of the house, they found Richard Ashton's Will. He had compensated both Campbell Kennedy's grandfather for his time, as well as Stephanie Carlson's mother. Since both had passed, Campbell and Stephanie were given the inheritance."

"That is wonderful. Too bad it was after the deaths of their relatives."

Jaxson shrugged. "I suppose they could ask Madam Criant to do a séance and contact their relatives to let them know they were not forgotten."

I chuckled. "I hope they do." I checked my watch. "It's six thirty on Christmas Eve. How about if I get ready and you pick me up in an hour? We can grab a bite to eat and then go back to your place. I will give you your present."

Iggy hopped up on the table. "You aren't going to leave me, are you?"

"I could never leave you. I was willing to go back in time just to be with you." And Jaxson, but I'd tell him that later.

"Okay."

"Come back to the apartment with me now. I bet Aimee

will want to say hi. I told her you were missing."

Iggy looked around. "Did the mistletoe make it back?"

"I don't know. It doesn't matter since I don't have any catnip, so I'm not sure how much good it will do you. Besides, that mistletoe seems to have caused more problems than I ever imagined."

He hung his head. "Okay."

I stood. "I'm going to say goodnight to Rihanna and wish her a wonderful Christmas Eve."

"I need to go back to my place to change. I'll pick you up in a bit," Jaxson said.

"Great."

Once he left, I checked to see if Rihanna was doing okay. When I opened the door, I stilled. My cousin was wearing a dark red velvet dress, and her hair was piled on top of her head. It kind of shocked me that she wasn't wearing black, and secondly, that she looked so grown up. Maybe traveling back in time had an effect on her. "Wow. You look stunning."

She spun around. "Do you think Gavin will like it?"

"I'm afraid he may like it a little too much."

She rolled her eyes. "Don't worry. We aren't at that point yet."

I wasn't exactly sure if she and I were talking about the same thing. "Just have fun. I'll see you tomorrow at my parents' house."

"You bet."

Iggy and I left for our apartment. As I walked over, I called my mom to tell her that Jaxson, Rihanna, and Iggy were safely back in Witch's Cove.

"That is wonderful. We'll see you and Rihanna tomorrow then?"

"Absolutely. Trust me, I won't be wishing on any coins in the near future."

"Good."

I disconnected and hurried in through the back entrance to the restaurant. Once inside my place, I suggested Iggy go see his girlfriend. I needed to take a modern shower and then dress for a romantic dinner and evening, and it would be easier without Iggy around.

Being in my own place was divine. Because I stayed in the shower longer than I should have, I was running a little late. I had planned to wear a pair of pink silk trousers and a pale pink blouse, but after seeing how amazing Rihanna looked, I decided to choose something a bit different—assuming I had anything off-color.

I found a print dress that had pink, purple and green flowers on it. The cut was form-fitting, which I was sure would appeal to Jaxson. After making certain I had my present and coat ready to go, I stepped across the hall to gather Iggy. He was welcome to join us, but if he chose to stay with Aimee, I was fine with it.

I knocked, but since Aunt Fern was most likely still at the party no one answered. Iggy hopped out of the cat door. "I'm going to stay with Aimee if that is okay with you."

"Sure. We're just going to watch some television anyway. You'd be bored."

"Uh-huh."

"Iggy Goodall."

"What? I know things."

I laughed. "Have fun and Merry Christmas Eve."

I returned to my apartment, gathered my things, and headed downstairs to wait for Jaxson.

Chapter Nineteen

ONCE WE RETURNED to Jaxson's place after an amazing dinner, he lit the fire and put on some soft music. I sighed. The food and company tonight had been outstanding, and I couldn't be happier.

"I know this will sound a little strange," I said, "But part of me misses Sissy's diner."

He laughed. "I hope I remember everything about that strange experience—all but the dismay at finding you gone."

I looked at him. "I never want to experience that panic again either. How about we open our presents?" I wasn't sure how Christmas Eve should go, but since he'd be leaving in the morning to visit his family, this was our only time to be together.

He pulled open a drawer in the coffee table, retrieved a small box, and handed it to me. "I hope you like it."

"I will love it." Considering the size, it looked to be jewelry of some sort.

About two weeks ago, we'd passed a jewelry storefront, and I'd commented on this gorgeous pink bracelet. I would be so thrilled if that was what he got me.

I carefully peeled back the paper, and then opened the box. My pulse soared as I lifted one of the earrings.

"What the heck?" Jaxson asked.

I stilled. "What's wrong?"

"That was not what I bought you."

"They're beautiful though." It was a pair of small gold coin earrings, each with a diamond in the middle. "You should return them. They are too expensive."

"I don't care about that. Can I see one?"

I handed it over to him. "There's an inscription on this coin. It's pretty small." He stood and moved closer to the fire, probably for better light.

I grabbed the other one and joined him. I tried to read the fine print. "Enjoy the past, but…"

"Live in the now," he continued.

"Wow. I like that, but it's a bit creepy."

Jaxson laughed. "How so?"

"It's like these earrings were meant to find me. Think about it. They are gold coins—just like the ones I wished on. And the diamonds? Yes, I know that is something men give women, but I've never worn anything like this before. It's as if one of the Ashton diamonds found its way here."

He whistled. "Is there a tag on the box to indicate which store it came from? I got this at Harold's Jewelry store—or at least I bought the pink bracelet you liked from there."

Aw. "I'll check." I lifted the box and turned it over. When I saw the name, I almost dropped it.

Jaxson was by my side in a flash. "What is it?"

"It says Baker and Baker Jewelers, Charlotte, Ohio."

He sat down on the sofa, and I joined him. "That's not possible. When the three of us returned, we were back in our old clothes. Nothing came with us."

"Nothing came back with me either."

"As much as I wish I had gotten you these earrings, I didn't buy them."

"Do you think the bracelet you got me is somewhere here?" I didn't want to sound ungrateful. "I only ask because I'd like to know if something magical is happening here."

He exhaled deeply. "I have no idea. How about I open my gift, and then I'll look?" He nodded to the box I'd placed on the coffee table.

"Okay." I handed it to him. I'd purchased a black, dressy button-down shirt. In addition, I included a pair of gold cufflinks. Together, Jaxson would look even more amazing than he already did.

He opened the box and pulled out a green, long sleeve cashmere sweater, just like the one he'd worn in Charlotte.

"I love it," he said. "I've never seen anything like this in the stores around here."

"That's…ah… because I didn't buy it either. I got you a black cotton shirt and some cufflinks."

He shook his head. "What is going on?"

"Maybe they are presents from Madam Criant."

Jaxson chuckled. "How is that possible? She's dead, right?"

"Yes. Then I'd have to say it's magic!"

He looked around. "I'm almost afraid all of this is going to disappear, and we'll end up someplace else."

"Or could this be a dream?"

"I doubt all four of us would have the same dream and the same memories?"

That did sound farfetched. I snapped my fingers. "We

could search to see what people say about time travel."

"I'm game, but I imagine most are kooks."

I had to laugh. "Don't you think people will believe we're crazy if we tell them what really happened?"

"You're right. Maybe we shouldn't tell anyone where we've been."

How quickly he forgot. "I just told the five gossip queens about our travels. I bet the whole town knows about it already."

Jaxson stabbed a hand through his hair. "That is a problem. I guess it's too late to deny it, right?"

"Whatever we say, we need Rihanna to agree."

Jaxson wrapped an arm around my shoulders. "How about that for tonight we forget about everything and concentrate on us?"

Who knew he could be so romantic? "That works for me."

"HOW WAS YOUR Christmas?" Jaxson asked the day after the big holiday.

"Good, but most of the time everyone just asked about our very strange experience."

"How did Dr. Sanchez respond to it? Being a medical professional, she doesn't truly believe in magic," he said.

"After that spell I did to cure Nash and Hunter, she's coming around." I held up a finger. "Speaking of our deputy, Nash came to Christmas dinner at my parents' house. Elissa invited him. Her in-laws were down in Miami visiting their son."

"Dr. Sanchez and Nash are a thing now?" Jaxson's brows rose.

"It seems so. After he was injured, and she helped save his life, I think things got interesting, shall we say. Mind you, they said very little about it probably because Gavin's mom wants to keep it on the down low." I chuckled. "I wish her the best with that. Witch's Cove is not the place to keep secrets."

"I won't say a word."

I leaned back. "Speaking of not saying a word, how much did you tell Drake and your parents about our experience?"

"Drake knows all. My parents? We thought it better to let it be."

I was so happy that I had parents who understood. "Maybe someday."

"Maybe." He pressed his lips together. "I got you something since I couldn't find the one I thought I bought."

My heart skipped a beat. "You didn't."

Jaxson smiled. "I did." He handed me the box. "Open it."

Inside was that gorgeous pink bracelet that I had coveted. I slipped it over my wrist. "It's perfect. Thank you!" I snapped my fingers. "I was luckier. For some reason, I found the box I'd purchased. The strange part was that it was wrapped in the identical paper and everything."

I gave it to him. Jaxson ripped opened the box and lifted out the shirt and cufflinks. "Oh, Glinda. It's perfect. Thank you." He tapped the cufflinks. "Do you know, I've never owned a pair?"

"Really? Then I'm glad you have some now."

He leaned over to give me a kiss when someone knocked

on our office door. I broke our brief contact. "Are you expecting anyone?" I asked.

"No."

It would be too good to be true to find out it was a client. We both stood, and I stepped over to the door to open it. A nice-looking man in his mid-thirties was there. "How can I help you?"

"Are you Glinda Goodall?"

"I am. Come in."

The man entered and looked around. When he spotted Jaxson, he smiled. "Are you Jason?"

"Ah, it's Jaxson."

"Yes, yes. I apologize. How about Rihanna? Is she here?"

How did he know about her? My protective side flared. "Who are you?"

"I am so sorry. I'm Quade Phillips. My grandmother was Bethany Criant."

I reached out to find something to steady myself. Thankfully, Jaxson took my hand.

"Let's all sit down," Jaxson said. "This is a little strange."

Quade nodded. "I bet it is. I have to say I wasn't sure I would ever find you."

"I'll get Rihanna," I said.

Just as I turned toward her room, she stepped into the main office area. She and Quade stared at each other, and I had to say it was a bit creepy. I'd seen that look before. She was reading his mind, and from what I could tell, he was doing the same thing.

Rihanna smiled. "I can't believe it. You are her grandson."

Quade laughed. "Yes. I was prepared to show you my

birth certificate."

My mind was unable to comprehend most of what was going on. "Are you from now or…then?"

"Now. I was born in 1985."

That made me feel a little better. "Where are you from?"

"All over the place, but I grew up in Charlotte. That was where I would hear the stories about the people who came from the future."

"Did that mean we were the only ones?"

He nodded. "As far as I know."

"I'm surprised your grandmother so readily believed us."

"She was a remarkable woman and a great psychic."

I swore Rihanna sighed. I wonder if that was what she aspired to be. "Do you know if your grandmother was the one who sent me the coin three times?"

"Yes. She talks about Gertrude Poole so much, I think she believed this was her way of connecting with her."

"Then why not time travel with Gertrude's grandson, Levy? I'm not related to Gertrude in any way."

Quade looked over at Rihanna. "Because of her."

"Me?" Rihanna said.

"Gertrude talked about you so much that my grandmother wanted to meet you. I know, it was after she'd passed, but the two had a powerful connection even in the afterlife. It was why she brought you back to her time. And then there was Iggy."

As if he'd been summoned, Iggy crawled out from under the sofa. "She talked about me?" he asked.

Quade's eyes widened. "She did." He studied Iggy. "My, but you are a handsome young man."

Oh, boy. He was laying it on a bit thick. Iggy was already impossible to live with since he'd been the one to find the diamonds that cracked the case.

"How did you find us?" Jaxson asked.

"I can communicate with my grandmother. She knew that Gertrude lived in Witch's Cove. It was a matter of asking at the local diner to learn what I wanted to know."

"This is all so unbelievable," I said. "I still can't comprehend that what happened was real."

He chuckled. "I get it. What I would give to be able to go back in time and visit my grandmother again."

I could totally understand that. "It was interesting, but getting back was a bit difficult, at least for Jaxson, Rihanna, and Iggy."

He lifted his jacket lapel and extracted an envelope. "About that. My grandmother had a devilish streak. She purposefully wanted one of you to return so that the others would do what she wanted."

Jaxson stiffened. "She really wanted those stock tips from the future?"

"Apparently, but trust me, I had no idea that they came from you until she was close to dying. My father knew, but I didn't."

"I don't understand," I said. Actually, I wasn't sure I understood how any of this would be true, despite the fact I am a witch, and I'd been the one to make the wish on the stupid coin in the first place.

"You gave my grandmother a list of three stocks that you said would be worth a lot someday."

"Yes. It was the only way we had a chance to get back to

our time."

Quade nodded. "My father took grandmother's advice and made a killing in the market. I am now a trader, too."

"I wonder if anyone would call that insider trading," I said.

"You don't work for those companies, so no. Besides, I sincerely doubt anyone could prove anything anyway." He waved the envelope. "That's why my family and I want you to have this. I know that starting a company needs capital. If it weren't for you, I would not have enjoyed the lifestyle I now have."

I looked over at Jaxson. He nodded. Since he was sitting next to me, I opened it. The number of zeros took my breath away. "This is too much. We can't accept this."

Quade held up his hand. "Consider it guilt money. My father has never felt right about it. Besides, you made my grandmother very happy. She was able to help return you to your Witch's Cove family."

Wasn't she the one who took us away in the first place? I might have said that, but I saw no point. This money would allow Jaxson the freedom to do what he enjoyed the most. Do research. "Saying thank you seems too little."

"Then how about dinner so we can get to know each other better."

I looked over at my coworkers.

"Can I come?" Iggy said.

We all laughed. "Absolutely."

Chapter Twenty

One month later.

RIHANNA HAD RETURNED to school, anxious to complete her senior year. Even though her mother was now out of rehab, my cousin said there weren't a lot of good memories in Jacksonville where her mom lived. She had tried to convince her to move here, but so far Aunt Tricia hadn't agreed. I was hoping she'd change her mind someday.

"You know what we forgot to ask Quade?" I asked.

Jaxson's brows rose. "What's that?"

"Whatever happened to the Ashton B&B. Did it stay as a Bed and Breakfast or did the city take it over and convert it into a museum?"

"I imagine that would be easy enough to investigate."

"We should. Do you think about our time there very often?" I asked.

Jaxson swiveled around in his chair. "Why all of the questions?"

I shrugged. "I don't know. It seems as if what happened to us changed us somehow."

"Changed? How?"

"The massive influx on capital from Quade aside, I think it helped the four of us grow closer."

Jaxson smiled, pushed back his chair, and stood. He came over to where I was straightening the sofa. We really needed a better one since this seemed to move on the floor too much.

He clasped me by the waist and turned me around. "I like closer."

I laughed. "I know you do. You are the more romantic between the two of us."

"That's because I don't have your analytic brain."

"Are you saying I'm smarter?"

He shook his head. "You know better than to ask."

I did know better. I was just about to kiss him when my stomach grumbled.

Jaxson's eyes widened. "Look at the clock. It's two past feeding time."

I stepped out of his embrace and punched his arm. He did love to kid me. "I wouldn't turn you down if you wanted to grab a bite to eat."

"Works for me."

Iggy was back at the apartment, so it was just the two of us. "What's your pleasure?"

"How about the Magic Wand Hotel?"

We rarely ate there mostly because it was so easy to stop at either the Spellbound Diner or the Tiki Hut Grill. The hotel food, while very good, was also more expensive. But hey, we could afford it.

We grabbed our jackets and headed out. The traffic was rather heavy since it was tourist season. When the stoplight turned red, it was our turn to cross.

In the middle of the road sat a gold coin. Jaxson stopped and bent over.

"Don't you dare pick that up!" I nearly shouted.

"Why not?"

"Are you kidding? I'm not taking any more chances on wish coins. Let's let someone else have that experience."

Jaxson held up his hands in defeat, pulled me to him, and ushered me across the street. Once on the other side, he turned to face me. "Glinda, life with you is never dull. I do adore you."

That made my heart sing. "And I you."

Okay, I'll admit it. I sighed.

Life in Witch's Cove was exactly where I wanted to be.

I hope you had as much fun going back in time as I did in writing it. I went to college in Ohio in the 70s. Don't worry, I changed the names to protect the innocent. In book 9, The Pink Iguana Sleuths have their hands full again. The father of someone dear to them is murdered by some powerful magical being. Our crew has to travel to Miami to unravel the mystery. I've included the first chapter of THE MAGICAL PINK PENDANT.

Buy on Amazon or read for FREE on Kindle Unlimited

Don't forget to sign up for my Cozy Mystery newsletter to learn about my discounts and upcoming releases. If you prefer to only receive notices regarding my releases, follow me on BookBub.
http://smarturl.it/VellaDayNL
bookbub.com/authors/vella-day

Here is a sneak peak of The Magical Pink Pendant

THE HARD POUNDING footsteps racing up the outside staircase of our Pink Iguana Sleuths' office caused a rush of hope to surge through me. This could be a paying customer! While my business partner—turned boyfriend—and I were no longer desperate for funds, I needed something to keep me mentally engaged. While I liked my former job as a waitress, it didn't stimulate my math brain like solving a murder did.

Before I had time to even push back my chair from my

computer desk, Gavin Sanchez, my cousin's new beau, slammed open the door. While the nineteen-year old normally acted in control, right now, he looked scared and rather confused.

"Is Rihanna here?" His words gushed out, and my heart broke at his distress.

Before I could tell him, Rihanna was in her room, she ran out and stopped dead in her tracks. "Gavin, what's wrong?" Her voice cracked.

"My father is…dead." He waved his arms, looking as if he punched the air hard enough, answers would miraculously appear.

His shocking statement had every cell in my body freezing. "What? He's dead? How?"

Rihanna had the sense to hug her boyfriend and then lead him over to the sofa. I was glad she didn't escort him into our newly-converted storage room turned bedroom since nosy me wanted all of the details.

I know it might seem strange that my eighteen-year old cousin, Rihanna Samuels, would be living at an office, but until she graduated from high school in a few months, she would be staying with us here—or longer if she so chose. Having her around made my life a bit more complete.

"I'll get you something to drink." The part of me that used to be a waitress often took over in a crisis.

Since Gavin frequently stopped over, I knew which soda he preferred. I fixed one for him, as well as a sweet tea for both me and Rihanna. Not wanting to miss even a word of this tragedy, I hurried.

Let me mention that I, Glinda Goodall, run a sleuth

agency with Jaxson Harrison, because…well…being a busybody is in my nature—as is being a witch.

I carried the drinks into the main room, placed them on the coffee table, and then sat across from them. "When you're ready, tell me what happened."

Gavin sat up straighter, his gaze bouncing around the room. Clearly, he was in shock, as anyone would be upon learning his not-very-old dad was dead. Poor guy. Gavin was already living under the stress of interning with his medical examiner mother. Having to deal with the death of a parent would crush anyone.

When he finally seemed to get himself under control, he faced both of us and blew out a breath. "Okay. Here goes. Nash got a call earlier this morning about a body in the backyard of our neighbor's house. Since the victim—my dad—wasn't carrying his wallet or anything, Nash had no idea who this person was, which meant he had to run a fingerprint scan."

"That must have come as a shock to our deputy." I couldn't imagine how hard it would be to tell your girlfriend that her former husband was dead.

"Nash said he was upset, which was why he asked the sheriff to double-check his findings."

"That makes sense." Considering where his dad was found, the sleuth in me immediately suspected foul play. "Who's backyard?"

"Mrs. Prentiss'."

"She's in her eighties." I didn't believe she'd be capable of harming a man in his prime.

"She is. Here's the bizarre part. Dad had been renting a

room from her for the last three days."

I couldn't help but suck in a breath at that news. First off, his Miami-based father was supposedly quite wealthy. I would have thought he'd have stayed in the Magic Wand Hotel, our nicest facility, rather than rent a room in someone's slightly rundown home.

"I take it, you didn't know he was in town?" If Gavin or Elissa had been aware of the dad's visit, they would have suggested a better place—or maybe that would have been my reaction.

Gavin shook his head and then sipped his drink. "Mom had no idea he was here. When we'd Skyped, Dad never mentioned any plans to see me either. The last time we chatted, all he could talk about was his upcoming trip to Rome with *Morgana*."

The emphasis on that name implied she wasn't high on Gavin's list of favorite people.

"Morgana is his new wife, right?" He'd mentioned her before, but clearly, I hadn't paid enough attention.

"Yes."

"Do you talk to your dad often?" It was important to understand how close they were.

"He'd set up a time most weeks to connect via Skype, but too often something would come up, and he'd have to cancel." Gavin shrugged, pretending it was no big deal, but the disappointment slicing across his face said otherwise.

"Lawyers are busy people." I hoped that would make him feel better. Doctors were busy, too, but I bet his mom would never cancel on him like that—or at least not very often.

"So he kept telling me." Gavin pressed his lips together.

"Do you have any idea what business he had in Witch's Cove, or why he didn't tell you he was here?" Rihanna asked.

"No, and it's not like Dad not to mention something that important. He never kept secrets from us."

None that they knew of. While this might not be a paying job for Jaxson and me, for my cousin's sake, I had to do what I could to help.

"What did your step-mother say about his visit here?" Despite some tension between them, I hoped Gavin had spoken with her.

"Morgana was as surprised as we were. My dad told her that he was going to Tallahassee for some lawyer's convention." His voice trembled, but I couldn't tell if it was from anger, frustration, or sadness.

If Mr. Sanchez lied to his new wife and son, he was hiding something. Only what?

Before I could come up with a list of possibilities, the office door opened. When Jaxson came in and smiled at me, my tight muscles relaxed a bit. His presence and level-headedness always helped calm me.

He stopped short when he spotted Gavin. Jaxson looked back at me and then at the young couple. "What happened?"

While Jaxson wasn't a witch, he had a sixth sense about people. The fact Gavin and Rihanna were on the sofa talking to me probably clued him in that things were amiss. They usually preferred their privacy. "Grab a chair, and we'll fill you in."

He'd just sat down when Iggy, my fifteen-year old pink iguana familiar popped in through the cat door.

"I'm getting too old to be climbing that railing," he complained. "You need to put in an elevator for me." For effect, he expanded and contracted his tiny chest. I'm guessing it was to show us he was out of breath, but I knew a faker when I saw one.

The idea of an elevator for a nine-pound iguana was ridiculous, but knowing Jaxson, he'd probably try to rig up something just to make Iggy happy.

I patted my thigh. "Iggy, come over here. There's been a death."

Acting as if he hadn't just climbed a mountain, Iggy raced over. "Who died? Do we get the case?" he asked with too much enthusiasm.

I was thankful that Gavin couldn't hear him—only witches and those who'd had a spell put on them could, like Jaxson. However, Rihanna had explained to Gavin that the rest of us could communicate with my ego-driven, talking lizard.

"Gavin's father," I whispered. I lifted him up onto my lap and pressed a finger to his mouth. Iggy could say some insensitive things at times, which wasn't cool.

"Is he asking about my dad?" Gavin nodded to my familiar.

"Yes." I didn't think translating what Iggy said would be helpful. "Rihanna, how about bringing Jaxson and Iggy up to speed?"

She outlined the series of events—or at least as much as she knew.

"How did he die?" Jaxson asked.

"I don't know," Gavin said. "It wasn't anything obvious like a gunshot wound or a blow to the head. Mom called in another medical examiner from Ocean View to do the autopsy. She'll just assist." He held up a hand. "It was actually Nash's idea that she not do it by herself, considering it's Dad."

I was actually surprised she was allowed to do anything relating to the body. Normally, those close to the deceased were suspects. I hope having Dr. Sanchez as his girlfriend didn't color his decision.

"Do you know when he died?" Jaxson asked.

"Nash and Mom thought sometime around two this morning."

I wanted to ask where his mother was at the time of Gavin's father's death, but it wasn't my place. If confronted, she'd say she was home in bed, which was probably true. If Nash was allowing her to handle the body, he must not think she was guilty in any way.

"Did your mom say if he'd been ill?" I asked. "His death could be from natural causes."

"No. As far as we know, Dad was healthy."

"Does your mom think someone murdered him then?"

"She isn't saying, but Nash thinks so, only he isn't telling me why," Gavin said.

Considering she was the medical examiner, she wasn't prone to speculation, which was what I really admired about her. I let out a sigh. This must be terribly traumatic for Gavin. I had to say, the young man was holding up rather well. I'd be bawling my eyes out if anything happened to either of my parents.

At least Rihanna would be able to relate to Gavin since her father had been murdered five months ago.

"What can we do to help, Gavin?" Jaxson asked.

"Nothing. I didn't come here for that. I just needed to see

Rihanna and tell her what happened."

I could understand that. "Rihanna, why don't you take Gavin into your room where you'll have more privacy."

She nodded. As soon as they slipped into the bedroom and closed the door, I faced Jaxson. "I can't even imagine what Gavin is going through right now, but we need to do something."

"We'll help in any way we can as soon as we learn that Mr. Sanchez was murdered."

I picked up my tea and sipped it, my mind racing. "Why would Daniel Sanchez rent a room down the street from his ex-wife and son and then not contact them?"

"Maybe he was spying on them."

"Spying? Why?"

"I don't know. Perhaps he heard that Elissa was seeing someone, and Daniel wanted to make sure this man wouldn't be a bad influence on his son."

"That makes sense, but I would think Gavin would have given him the lowdown on Nash since Gavin and his dad were in regular contact. If Daniel didn't want to talk directly to his ex-wife about Nash, why not have Gavin meet him for dinner in town or something to discuss it?"

"Those are excellent questions," he said.

"I understand wanting to check out Nash, but staying a few doors down the street is almost asking to be spotted."

"For sure."

"Forgetting why Donald Sanchez was in town or the reason for staying so close to the ex-wife, why would someone want him dead? I don't recall hearing he'd even been to Witch's Cove in a long time even though his parents live here."

Jaxson huffed. "I have no idea, but didn't you tell me he'd recently remarried?"

"Yes."

"Maybe the new wife thought he wanted to get back with his ex-wife and ordered a hit on him. Trouble in paradise is often a good motive for murder."

I held up a finger at his wild imagination. Having crazy hypotheses were usually up my alley. "Mrs. Sanchez claimed she didn't know he was here."

"People lie."

"True. It's possible either Daniel came to Witch's Cove to make amends with Elissa, or because their divorce had been so contentious that he wanted to clear the air in order to get a fresh start with his new wife. When he spotted Elissa cozying up to our deputy, Daniel might have decided to sit back and watch before making his move."

"Could very well be. That might explain why he didn't meet his son. He didn't want Gavin to tip off Elissa that he was in town," Jaxson said.

"Too bad all of these theories are pure conjecture. But you know who might have the deets on what really happened between our good medical examiner and her former husband?"

"Pearl?"

Pearl Dillsmith was the sheriff department's receptionist. She kept the job in her old age mostly because her grandson was now the sheriff.

"Precisely," I said. "If Pearl is privy to what could have happened, her best buddy Dolly would have gotten the lowdown by now, too."

Jaxson rubbed his stomach. "I'm so hungry."

He was mocking me. "You can just say we need to go to the diner in order to talk to Dolly. There's no need for the hunger ruse. You know I'm always up for eating."

Jaxson chuckled, as I'd hoped.

Iggy looked up at me. "Can I come?"

"You know it's hard to talk to you without looking like I'm crazy, and when I don't speak to you, you can get huffy."

"Me? Huffy? I'm a model citizen."

"Sure, you are." I cleared my throat. "I think you'd be better off spying on the two teens."

He lifted his chest. "Spy? Me? I never would do that."

"I wasn't born yesterday." His favorite pastime was listening to conversations—especially private ones.

Iggy dropped onto his stomach. "Fine. What's your best bet on the motive for killing this guy? Greed, revenge, or jealousy?"

"Let's not jump to any conclusions. We don't know that he didn't die from natural causes."

"But suppose he was killed?" Iggy asked.

"Fine. I'd go with jealousy." I honestly had no idea, but Iggy would keep bugging me unless I picked one.

Iggy bounced up and down. "That sounds juicy."

I wagged a finger at him. "Juicy, maybe, but not substantiated. We probably should rule out revenge, though." I was only kidding. I never eliminated any motive until I had proof—at least most of the time I didn't.

"Why?" Jaxson asked, clearly not understanding I wasn't serious. "Gavin's dad was a lawyer. Perhaps one of his clients was convicted due to Sanchez's poor handling of the man's case. If he'd recently completed his sentence, he'd be free to come after him."

I sunk back against the chair. "According to Gavin, his dad won most of his cases, implying he was a good lawyer. In case he did mess up, this opens up a whole slew of suspects."

"The sad part is that we can't eliminate anyone who is still in jail. When I served time for my bogus crime, too often I'd hear stories about an inmate hiring someone to exact revenge for him."

"That stinks. What's worse is that the suspects are probably still in Miami, which is a huge town." At least when a murder happened in Witch's Cove, it was moderately easy to keep track of their comings and goings. We had eyes and ears everywhere.

"How about we let Iggy do his magic with the teens, and you and I hit up the Spellbound Diner? You know Dolly will be on top of things, what with Pearl on the case," Jaxson said.

"I love a good plan." And something sweet to eat.

Buy on Amazon or read for FREE on Kindle Unlimited

THE END

A WITCH'S COVE MYSTERY (Paranormal Cozy Mystery)
PINK Is The New Black (book 1)
A PINK Potion Gone Wrong (book 2)
The Mystery of the PINK Aura (book 3)
Box Set (books 1-3)
Sleuthing In The PINK (book 4)
Not in The PINK (book 5)
Gone in the PINK of an Eye (book 6)
Box Set (books 4-6)
The PINK Pumpkin Party (book 7)
Mistletoe with a PINK Bow (book 8)
The Magical PINK Pendant (book 9)
The Poisoned PINK Punch (book 10)

SILVER LAKE SERIES (3 OF THEM)
(1). **HIDDEN REALMS OF SILVER LAKE** (Paranormal Romance)
Awakened By Flames (book 1)
Seduced By Flames (book 2)
Kissed By Flames (book 3)
Destiny In Flames (book 4)
Box Set (books 1-4)
Passionate Flames (book 5)
Ignited By Flames (book 6)
Touched By Flames (book 7)
Box Set (books 5-7)
Bound By Flames (book 8)
Fueled By Flames (book 9)
Scorched By Flames (book 10)

(2). FOUR SISTERS OF FATE: HIDDEN REALMS OF SILVER LAKE (Paranormal Romance)

Poppy (book 1)
Primrose (book 2)
Acacia (book 3)
Magnolia (book 4)
Box Set (books 1-4)
Jace (book 5)
Tanner (book 6)

(3). WERES AND WITCHES OF SILVER LAKE

(Paranormal Romance)
A Magical Shift (book 1)
Catching Her Bear (book 2)
Surge of Magic (book 3)
The Bear's Forbidden Wolf (book 4)
Her Reluctant Bear (book 5)
Freeing His Tiger (book 6)
Protecting His Wolf (book 7)
Waking His Bear (book 8)
Melting Her Wolf's Heart (book 9)
Her Wolf's Guarded Heart (book 10)
His Rogue Bear (book 11)
Box Set (books 1-4)
Box Set (books 5-8)
Reawakening Their Bears (book 12)

OTHER PARANORMAL SERIES
PACK WARS (Paranormal Romance)
Training Their Mate (book 1)
Claiming Their Mate (book 2)
Rescuing Their Virgin Mate (book 3)
Box Set (books 1-3)
Loving Their Vixen Mate (book 4)
Fighting For Their Mate (book 5)
Enticing Their Mate (book 6)
Box Set (books 1-4)
Complete Box Set (books 1-6)

HIDDEN HILLS SHIFTERS (Paranormal Romance)
An Unexpected Diversion (book 1)
Bare Instincts (book 2)
Shifting Destinies (book 3)
Embracing Fate (book 4)
Promises Unbroken (book 5)
Bare 'N Dirty (book 6)
Hidden Hills Shifters Complete Box Set (books 1-6)

CONTEMPORARY SERIES
MONTANA PROMISES (Full length contemporary Romance)
Promises of Mercy (book 1)
Foundations For Three (book 2)
Montana Fire (book 3)
Montana Promises Box Set (books 1-3)
Hart To Hart (Book 4)
Burning Seduction (Book 5)
Montana Promises Complete Box Set (books 1-5)

ROCK HARD, MONTANA (contemporary romance novellas)
Montana Desire (book 1)
Awakening Passions (book 2)

PLEDGED TO PROTECT (contemporary romantic suspense)
From Panic To Passion (book 1)
From Danger To Desire (book 2)
From Terror To Temptation (book 3)
Pledged To Protect Box Set (books 1-3)

BURIED SERIES (contemporary romantic suspense)
Buried Alive (book 1)
Buried Secrets (book 2)
Buried Deep (book 3)
The Buried Series Complete Box Set (books 1-3)

A NASH MYSTERY (Contemporary Romance)
Sidearms and Silk (book 1)
Black Ops and Lingerie (book 2)
A Nash Mystery Box Set (books 1-2)

STARTER SETS (Romance)
Contemporary
Paranormal

Author Bio

Love it HOT and STEAMY? Sign up for my newsletter and receive MONTANA DESIRE for FREE. smarturl.it/o4cz93?IQid=MLite

OR Are you a fan of quirky PARANORMAL COZY MYSTERIES? Sign up for this newsletter. smarturl.it/CozyNL

Not only do I love to read, write, and dream, I'm an extrovert. I enjoy being around people and am always trying to understand what makes them tick. Not only must my romance books have a happily ever after, I need characters I can relate to. My men are wonderful, dynamic, smart, strong, and the best lovers in the world (of course).

My Paranormal Cozy Mysteries are where I let my imagination run wild with witches and a talking pink iguana who believes he's a real sleuth.

I believe I am the luckiest woman. I do what I love and I have a wonderful, supportive husband, who happens to be hot!

Fun facts about me

(1) I'm a math nerd who loves spreadsheets. Give me numbers and I'll find a pattern.
(2) I live on a Costa Rica beach!
(3) I also like to exercise. Yes, I know I'm odd.

I love hearing from readers either on FB or via email (hint, hint).

Social Media Sites

Website:
www.velladay.com

FB:
facebook.com/vella.day.90

Twitter:
@velladay4

Gmail:
velladayauthor@gmail.com